'Of all serious science fiction writers A. E. van Vogt is the most promising. He s  all the richest themes of the g f space travel, the strang d life in other stellar sy d the vast possibilities s Wilson in The Observ

'A. E. van Vogt is one of the enduring primitives....If you haven't yet tried him, you should.' *Edmund Cooper* in *The Sunday Times*

* *Moonbeast* was originally entitled *The Beast*

Also by A. E. van Vogt

A. E. van Vogt

Moonbeast

PANTHER
GRANADA PUBLISHING
London Toronto Sydney New York

Published by Granada Publishing Limited
in Panther Books 1969
Reprinted 1970, 1973, 1975, 1978

ISBN 0 586 02937 0

First published in Great Britain by
Sidgwick & Jackson Ltd (as 'The Beast'
in *A van Vogt Omnibus*) 1967
Copyright © A. E. van Vogt 1943, 1944, 1963

Granada Publishing Limited
Frogmore, St Albans, Herts AL2 2NF
and
3 Upper James Street, London W1R 4BP
1221 Avenue of the Americas, New York, NY 10020, USA
117 York Street, Sydney, NSW 2000, Australia
100 Skyway Avenue, Toronto, Ontario, Canada M9W 3A6
110 Northpark Centre, 2193 Johannesburg, South Africa
CML Centre, Queen & Wyndham, Auckland 1, New Zealand

Made and printed in Great Britain by
Richard Clay (The Chaucer Press) Ltd
Bungay, Suffolk
Set in Linotype Pilgrim

Moonbeast

One

The blue-gray engine lay almost buried in a green hillside. It lay there in that summer of 1972, a soulless thing of metal and of forces almost as potent as life itself. Rain washed its senseless form. A July, then an August sun blazed down on it. At night the stars reflected wanly from the metal, caring nothing for its destiny. The ship it drove had been nosing down into Earth's atmosphere when the meteorite plowed through the block that held it in place. Instantly, with irresistible strength, the engine tore to shreds what remained of the framework and plunged through the gaping meteorite hole, down, down.

For all the weeks since then it had lain on the hillside, seemingly lifeless, but actually in its great fashion alive. There was dirt in its force field, so hard-packed that it would have taken special perception to see how swiftly it was spinning. Not even the boys who sat one day on a flange of the engine noticed the convulsions of the dirt. If one of them had poked a grimy hand into the inferno of energy that was the force field, muscles, bones, blood would have spurted like gas exploding.

But the boys went away, and the engine was still there on the afternoon the searchers passed along the bottom of the hill. Discovery was as close as that. There were two of them, perhaps a little tired at the late hour, yet trained observers nonetheless, who anxiously scanned the hillside. But a cloud was veiling the brightness of the sun, and they passed on, unseeing.

It was more than a week later, again late in the day, when a horse climbing the hill straddled the protruding bulge of the engine. The horse's rider proceeded to dismount in an astounding fashion. With his one hand he grasped the saddlehorn and *lifted* himself clear of the saddle. Casually, easily, be brought his left leg over, held himself poised in midair, and then dropped to the ground. The display of strength seemed all the more effortless because the action was automatic. His attention was concentrated the whole while on the thing on the ground.

His lean face twisted as he examined the machine. He glanced around, eyes narrowed. Then he smiled sardonically as he realized the thought in his mind. Finally he shrugged. There was little chance of anybody seeing him out here. The town of Crescentville was more than a mile away, and there was no sign of life around the big white house which stood among the trees a third of a mile to the northeast.

He was alone with his horse and the machine. And after a moment his voice echoed with cool irony on the twilight air. 'Well, Dandy, here's a job for us. This scrap should buy you quite a bit of feed. We'll haul it to the junk dealer after dark. That way she won't find out and we'll save some remnant of our pride.'

He stopped. Involuntarily he turned to stare at the garden-like estate whose width stretched for nearly a mile between himself and the town. A white fence, misty and halo-like in the twilight, made a vast circuit around a verdant land of trees and pasture. The fence kept disappearing down gullies and into brush. It vanished finally in the north beyond the stately white house.

The man muttered impatiently, 'What a fool I've been, hanging around Crescentville waiting for her.' He turned to stare down at the engine. 'Have to get some idea of its weight,' he thought. Then : 'Wonder what it is.'

He climbed to the top of the hill and came down again, carrying a piece of deadwood about four feet long and three inches in diameter. He began to pry the engine loose from the ground. It was awkward work with only a left arm. And so, when he noticed the dirt-plugged hole in the center, he jabbed the wood into it to get a better leverage.

His shout of surprise and pain echoed hoarsely on the evening air.

For the wood jerked. Like a shot twisted by the rifled barrel of a gun, like a churning knife, it wrenched in his hand, tearing like a shredder, burning like fire. He was lifted up, up, and flung twenty feet down the hill. Groaning, clutching his tattered hand to his body, he stumbled to his feet.

The sound died on his lips then as his gaze fastened on the throbbing, whirling thing that had been a dead branch of tree. He stared. Then he climbed, trembling, onto the black horse. Nursing his bloodied hand, blinking from the agony, he raced the animal down the hill and toward the highway that led to the town.

A stoneboat and harness for Dandy rented from a farmer, rope and tackle, a hand stiff with bandages, still numb with pain, a trek through darkness with a thrumming thing on the sled—for three hours Pendrake felt himself a creature in a nightmare.

But here was the engine now, on the floor of his stable, safe from discovery except for the sound that was pouring forth from the wood in its force field. It seemed odd now how his mind had worked. The determination to transport the engine secretly to his own cottage had been like choosing life instead of death, like swiftly picking up a hundred-dollar bill lying on a deserted street, so automatic as to be beyond the need of logic. It still seemed as natural as living.

The yellow glow from the lantern filled the interior of what had once been a private garage and workshop. In one corner Dandy stood, black hide aglint, eyes glistening as he turned his head to stare at the thing that shared his quarters. The not unpleasant smell of horse was thick now that the door was closed. The engine lay on its side near the door. And the main trouble was that the wood in it wasn't straight. It slogged away against the air like some caricature of a propeller, beating a sound out of the atmosphere by the sheer violence and velocity of its rotation.

Pendrake estimated its speed at about four thousand revolutions a minute. He stood then and strove to grasp the nature of a machine that could snatch a piece of wood and spin it so violently. The thought got nowhere. The frown on his face deepened as he stared down at the speed-blurred wood. He couldn't simply grab it. And, while undoubtedly there were a number of tools in the world that might grip a whirling object and pull on it, they were not available here in this lantern-lighted stable.

He thought: 'There must be a control, something to switch off the power.'

But the bluish-gray, doughnut-shaped outer shell was glass-smooth. Even the flanges that projected from four ends and in which were the holes for bed bolts seemed to grow out of the shell, as if they had been molded from the same block of metal, as if there had been a flowing, original design that spurned anything less than oneness. Baffled, Pendrake walked around the machine. It seemed to him that the problem was beyond the solution of a man who had as his working equipment one badly maimed and bandaged hand.

He noticed something. The machine lay solidly, heavily, on the floor. It neither jogged nor jumped. It made not the slightest effort to begin a sedate, reactionary creep in opposition to the insanely whirling thing that bristled from its middle. The engine was ignoring the law that action and reaction are equal and opposite.

With abrupt realization of the possibilities. Pendrake bent down and heaved at the metal shell. Instantly knives of pain hacked at his hand. Tears shocked into his eyes. But when he finally let go, the engine was standing on one of its four sets of flanges. And the crooked wood was spinning, no longer vertically, but roughly horizontal to the floor.

The pulse of agony in Pendrake's hand slowed. He wiped the tears from his eyes and proceeded to the next step in the plan that had occurred to him. Nails! He drove them into the bed bolts and bent them over the metal. That was merely to make sure that the narrow-based engine wouldn't topple over in the event that he bumped too hard against the outer shell.

An apple box came next. Laid lengthwise on its side, it reached up to within half an inch of the exact center of the large hole, from the opposite side of which the wood projected. Two books held steady a piece of one-inch piping about a foot long. It was painful holding the small sledge hammer in that lame hand of his, but he struck true. The piece of piping recoiled from the hammer, banged the wood where it was held inside the hole of the engine, and knocked it out.

There was a crash that shook the garage. After a moment Pendrake grew aware of a long, splintered slash in the ceiling, through which the four-foot piece of deadwood had bounced after striking the floor. Slowly his reverberating mind gravitated into a rhythm with the silence that was settling. Pendrake drew a deep breath. There were still things to discover, a whole new machine world to explore. But one thing seemed clear:

He had conquered the engine.

At midnight he was still awake. He kept getting up, dropping the magazine he was reading, and going into the dark kitchen of the cottage to peer out at the darker garage. But the night was quiet. No marauders disturbed the peace of the town. Occasionally a car motor sounded far away.

He began to realize the psychological danger when for the dozenth time he found himself pressing his face against the cool pane of the kitchen window. Pendrake cursed aloud and went back into the living room. What was he trying to do? He couldn't hope to keep that engine. It must be a new invention, a radical postwar development, lying on that hillside because of an accident a silly ass who never read papers or listened to the radio wouldn't know anything about.

Somewhere in the house, he remembered, was a *New York Times* he'd bought not so long ago. He found the paper in his magazine rack with all the other old and unread papers and magazines he'd bought from time to time. The date at the top was June 7, 1971, and this was August 16. Not too great a difference.

But this wasn't 1971. This was 1972.

With a cry Pendrake leaped to his feet, then slowly sank back into his chair. It was an ironic picture that came then, a kaleidoscope of the existence of a man so untouched by the friction of time that fourteen months had glided by like so many days. Lazy, miserable hound, Pendrake thought, using his lost arm and an unforgiving woman as an excuse for lying down on life. That was over. All of it. He'd start again. . . .

He grew aware of the paper in his hand. And the anger went out of him as in a gathering excitement he began to glance at the headlines:

PRESIDENT CALLS ON NATION
FOR NEW INDUSTRIAL EFFORT

TRILLION-DOLLAR NATIONAL INCOME
ONLY BEGINNING, JEFFERSON DAYLES SAYS

6,350,000 FAMILY JET TRAILERS SOLD
FIRST FIVE MONTHS OF 1971

It occurred to Pendrake at that point that the situation was that he had crept away into this little cottage of his, almost right out of the world, but that life had gone on dynamically. And somewhere, not so long ago, a tremendous invention had spawned out of that surging tide of will and ambition and creative genius. Tomorrow he would try to get a mortgage on this cottage. That would provide him with a little cash and break forever the thrall of the place. Dandy he'd send over to Eleanor in the same fashion that she had sent him three years ago, without a word. The green pastures of the estate would be like heaven for an animal that had starved too long now on an ex-pilot's pension.

He must have slept, with that thought. Because he awoke at 3 a.m., sweating with fear. He was out in the night and clawing open the door of the garage-stable before he realized that he had had a bad dream. The engine was still there, the foot-long piece of piping in its force field. In the beam of his flashlight the piping glinted as it turned, shone with a brown glow that was hard to reconcile with the dirty, rusted, extruded metal thing he had ransacked out of his basement.

It struck Pendrake after a moment, and for the first time, that the pipe was turning far more slowly than had the piece of wood, not a quarter so fast, not more than fourteen or fifteen hundred revolutions per minute. The rate of rotation must be governed by the kind of material, based on atomic weight, or density, or something.

Uneasily, convinced that he mustn't be seen abroad at this hour, Pendrake shut the door and returned to the house. He felt no anger at himself or at the brief frenzy that had sent him racing into the night. But the implications were troubling.

It was going to be hard to give up the engine to its rightful owner.

Two

The following day Pendrake went first to the office of the local newspaper. Forty issues of the weekly Crescentville *Clarion* yielded nothing. He read the first two pages of each edition, missing not a single heading. But there was no report of an air crash, no mention of a great new engine invention. He walked out finally into the hot August morning, exhilarated. Hard to believe. And yet, if this kept on, the engine was his.

From the newspaper office he went to the local branch of a national bank. The loan officer smiled at him faintly as he made his want known, and took him in to see the bank manager. The manager said, 'Mr. Pendrake, it isn't necessary for you to take a mortgage on your cottage. You have a large account here.'

He introduced himself as Roderick Clay and went on, 'As you know, when you went to Asia with the Army Air Force, you signed all your possessions over to your wife, with the exception of the cottage where you now live. And that, as I understand it, was omitted accidentally.'

Pendrake nodded, not trusting himself to speak. He knew now what was coming, and the manager's words merely verified his realization. The manager said, 'At the end of the war, a few months after you and your wife separated, she secretly reassigned to you the entire property, including bonds, shares, cash, real estate, as well as the Pendrake estate, with the stipulation that you not be advised of the transfer until you actually inquired or in some other fashion indicated your need for money. She further stipulated that, in the interim, she be given the minimum living allowance with which to provide for the maintenance of herself and the Pendrake home.

'I may say'—the man was bland, smug, satisfied with the way he had carried off an interview that he must have planned in his idle moments with anticipatory thrills—'your affairs have prospered with those of the nation. Stocks, bonds, and cash on hand total about one million two hundred and ninety-four thousand dollars. Would you like me to have one of the clerks prepare a check for your signature? How much?'

It was hotter outside. Pendrake walked back to the cottage, thinking: He should have known Eleanor would pull something like that. These intense, introverted, unforgiving women—— Sitting there that day he had called, cold, remote, unable to break out of her shell of reserve. Sitting there, knowing she had placed herself financially at his mercy. He'd have to think out what it might mean, plan his approach, his exact words and actions. Meanwhile, there was the engine.

It was exactly where he had left it. He glanced cursorily in at it, then padlocked the door again. On the way to the kitchen entrance he patted Dandy, who was staked out on the back lawn. Inside the cottage, he searched for, and found, the name of a Washington patent firm. He'd gone to Asia with the son of a member. Awkwardly he wrote his letter. On the way to the post office to mail it, he stopped off at the only machine shop in town and ordered a wheel-like gripping device, a sort of clutch, the wheel part of which would whirl with anything it grasped.

The answer to his letter arrived two days later, before the 'clutch' was completed. The letter said:

Dear Mr. Pendrake:

As per your request, we placed the available members of our Research Department on your problem. All the patent office records of engine inventions during the past three years were examined. In addition, I had a personal talk with the director in charge of that particular department of the patent office. Accordingly, I am in a position to state positively that no radical engine inventions other than jet variations have been patented in any field since the war.

For your perusal, we are enclosing herewith copies of ninety-seven recent engine patents, as selected by our staff from thousands.

Our bill is being sent to you by separate mail. Thank you for your advance check for two hundred dollars.

Sincerely yours,

N. V. HOSKINS

P.S. I thought you were dead. I'll swear I saw your name in a casualty list after I was rescued, and I've been mourning you ever since. I'll write you a long letter in a week or so. I'm holding up the patent world right now, not physically— only the great Jim Pendrake could do that. However, I'm playing the role of mental Atlas, and I sure got a lot of dirty looks for rushing your stuff through. Which explains the big bill. 'By for now.

NED

Pendrake was conscious of a choking sensation as he read and reread the note. It hurt him to think how he'd cut himself off from all his friends. The phrase 'the great Jim Pendrake' made him glance involuntarily at the empty right sleeve of his sweater.

He smiled grimly. And several minutes passed before he remembered the engine. He thought then, 'I'll order an automobile chassis and an engineless plane, and a bar made of many metals—have to make some tests first, of course.'

He stopped, his eyes widening at the possibilities. Life was opening up again. But it was strangely hard to realize that the engine still had no owner but himself.

Two days later he went to pick up the gripper. As he unfolded a tarpaulin to put around it, Pendrake heard a sound; then, 'What's that?' said a young man's voice behind him.

It was growing quite dark, and the truck he had hired seemed almost formless in the gathering night. Beside Pendrake the machine shop loomed, a gloomy, unpainted structure. The lights inside the building glimmered faintly through greasy windows. The machine-shop employees, who had loaded the gripper on the truck for him, were gone through a door, their raucous good nights still ringing in his ears. Pendrake was alone with his questioner.

With a deliberate yet swift movement he pulled the canvas over the gripper and turned to stare at the man who had addressed him. The fellow stood in the shadows, a tall, powerful-looking man. The light from the nearest street lamp glinted on high curving cheekbones, but it was hard to make out the exact contours of the face.

It was the intentness of the other's manner that sent a

chill through Pendrake. Here was no idler's curiosity, but an earnestness, a determination that was startlingly purposeful. With an effort Pendrake caught himself. 'What's it to you?' he said curtly.

He climbed into the cab. The engine purred. Awkwardly Pendrake manipulated the right-hand gear-control button, and the truck rolled off.

He could see the man in his rear-view mirror, still standing there in the shadows of the machine shop, a tall, strong figure. The stranger started to walk slowly in the same direction that Pendrake was driving. The next second Pendrake whipped the truck around a corner and headed down a side street. He thought, 'I'll take a roundabout course to the cottage and then quickly return the truck to the man I rented it from and then——'

Something damp trickled down his cheeks. He let go of the steering wheel and felt his face. It was covered with sweat. He sat very still, thinking: 'Am I crazy? Surely I don't believe that someone is secretly searching for the engine.'

His jumpy nerves slowly quieted. What was finally convincing was the coincidence of such a searcher standing near a machine shop of a small town at the very instant that Jim Pendrake was there. It was like an old melodrama in which the villains were dogging the unsuspecting hero. Ridiculous! Nevertheless, the episode emphasized an important aspect of his possession of the engine. Somewhere that engine had been built. Somewhere was the owner.

He must never forget that.

The darkness of the night had closed in when Pendrake finally entered the garage-stable and turned on the light he had installed earlier in the day. The two-hundred-watt bulb shed a sunlike glare that somehow made the small room even stranger than it had been by lantern light.

The engine stood exactly where he had nailed it that first night. It stood there like a swollen tire for a small, broad wheel; like a large, candied, blue-gray doughnut. Except for the four sets of flanges and the size, the resemblance to a doughnut was quite startling. The walls curved upward from the hole in the center; the hole itself was only a little smaller than it should have been to be in exact proportion. But there the resemblance to anything he had ever known ended. The hole was the damnedest thing that ever was.

It was about six inches in diameter. Its inner walls were smooth, translucent, non-metallic in appearance; and in its geometrical center floated the piece of plumber's pipe. Literally, the pipe hung in space, held in position by a force that seemed to have no origin.

Pendrake drew a deep, slow breath, picked up his hammer, and gently laid it over the outjutting end of the pipe. The hammer throbbed in his hand, but grimly he bore the pulsing needles of pain and pressed. The pipe whirred on, unyielding, unaffected. The hammer brrred with vibration. Pendrake grimaced from the agony and jerked the tool free.

He waited patiently until his hand ceased throbbing, then struck the protruding end of pipe a sharp blow. The pipe receded into the hole, and nine inches of it emerged from the other side of the engine. It was almost like rolling a ball. With deliberate aim, Pendrake hit the pipe from the far side. It bounced back so easily that eleven inches of it flowed out, only an inch remaining in the hole. It spun on like a shaft of a steam turbine, only there was not even a whisper of sound, not the faintest hiss.

With lips pursed, Pendrake sat on his heels. The engine was not perfect. The ease with which the pipe and, originally the piece of wood had been pushed in and out meant that gears or something would be needed. Something that would hold steady at high speeds under great strains. He climbed slowly to his feet, intent now. He dragged into position the device he had had constructed at the machine shop. It took several minutes to adjust the gripping wheel to the right height. But he was patient.

Finally he manipulated the control lever. Fascinated, he watched the two halves of the wheel close over the one-inch pipe, grip, and begin to spin. A glow suffused his whole body. It was the sweetest pleasure that had touched him in three long years. Gently Pendrake pulled on the gripping machine, tried to draw it toward him along the floor. It didn't budge. He frowned at it. He had the feeling that the machine was too heavy for delicate pressures. Muscle was needed here, and without restraint. Bracing himself, he began to tug, hard.

Afterward he remembered flinging himself back toward the door in his effort to get out of the way. He had a mental picture of the nails that held the engine to the floor pulling out as the engine toppled over toward him. The next instant the engine *lifted*, lifted lightly, in some incomprehensible fashion, right off the floor. It whirled there for a moment slowly, propeller-fashion, then fell heavily on top of the gripping machine.

With a crash the wooden planks on the floor splintered. The concrete underneath, the original floor of the garage, shattered with a grinding noise as the gripping machine was smashed against it fourteen hundred times a minute. Metal squealed in torment and broke into pieces in a shattering hail of death. The confusion of sound and dust and spraying concrete and metal was briefly a hideous environment for Pendrake's stunned mind.

Silence crept over the scene like the night following a day of battle, an intense, unnatural silence. There was blood on Dandy's quivering flank where something had gashed him. Pendrake stood, soothing the trembling horse, assessing the extent of the destruction. He saw that the engine was lying on its face, apparently unaffected by its own violence. It lay, a glinting, blue-gray thing, in the light from the miraculously untouched electric bulb.

It took half an hour to find all the pieces of what had been the gripping machine. He gathered the parts one by one and took them into the house. The first real experiment with the machine was over. Successfully, he decided.

He sat in darkness in the kitchen, watching. The minutes ticked by. And there was still no movement outside. Pendrake sighed finally. It seemed clear that no one had noticed the cataclysm in his garage. Or if they had, they were not curious. The engine was still safe.

The easing tension brought awareness of how lonely he was. Suddenly the very restfulness of the silence oppressed him. He had an abrupt, sharp conviction that his developing victory over the engine wasn't going to be any fun for one man cut off from the world by the melancholy of his character. He thought drably: 'I ought to go see her.'

No—that wouldn't work. Eleanor had acquired an emotional momentum in a given direction. It wouldn't do any good to go and see her. But there was another possibility.

Pendrake put on his hat and went out into the night. At the corner drugstore he headed straight for the phone booth. 'Is Mrs. Pendrake in?' he asked when his call was answered.

'Yes, suh!' The woman's deep voice indicated that there was at least one new servant at the big house. It was not a familiar voice. 'Just a moment, suh.'

A few seconds later Eleanor's rich contralto was saying, 'Mrs. Pendrake speaking.'

'Eleanor, this is Jim.'

'Yes?' Pendrake smiled wanly at the tiny change in her tone, the defensive edge that was suddenly in it.

'I'd like to come back, Eleanor,' he said softly.

There was silence, then——

Click!

Out in the night again, Pendrake looked up at the starry heavens. The sky was dark, dark blue. The whole fabric of the universe of Occidental earth was well settled into night. Crescentville shared with the entire eastern seaboard the penumbral shadows of the great mother planet. He thought: 'Maybe it was a mistake, but now she knows.' Her mind had probably gone dead slow on thoughts about him. Now it would come alive again.

He strolled up the back alley to his cottage. Reaching the yard, he suppressed an impulse to climb a tree from which the big white house was visible. He flung himself on the cool grass of the back lawn, stared at the garage, and thought shakily: An engine that spins anything shoved into its force field or, if it resisted, would smash it with the ease of power unlimited. An engine through which a shaft could be *pushed*, but from which it could not be *pulled*. Which meant that an airplane propeller need only to be fastened to a bar of graded metals—graded according to atomic weight and density.

Someone was knocking at the front door of the cottage. Pendrake jumped to his feet, instantly alarmed. But it was only a boy with a telegram which read:

'CABIN MODEL PUMA DELIVERED TO DORMANTOWN AIRPORT TOMORROW STOP SPECIAL ENGINE BRACES AND CONTROLS INSTALLED AS REQUESTED STOP MAGNESIUM ALLOY AND AEROGEL PLASTIC CONSTRUCTION STOP

ATLANTIC AIRCRAFT CORP.'

He was there the next day to take delivery. He had rented a hangar at the far end of the field, and he had the men on the big truck trailer unload the plane inside. When the delivery people were gone, he locked and bolted the doors. At dawn the following morning he drove the engine over and began the laborious task of installing it with the equipment he had bought for that purpose. It took time for one man with one arm, but he was persistent, and he completed the task. That night he slept in the hangar and was up as the first light of day glinted under the door. He had brought the makings of breakfast, and now he brewed himself some coffee and ate hastily. Then he opened the hangar doors and wheeled the plane out.

He made it a simple test flight, conservatively going no higher than 5000 feet and no faster than 175 miles per hour. It was disturbing to have no engine roar, so he came down uneasily, wondering if anyone had noticed. He surmised that even if it hadn't happened this time, sooner or later his machine in its silent journeyings would be remarked. And every day that passed, every hour that he clung to his secrecy, his moral position would grow worse. Somebody owned the engine. Owned it and wanted it. He must decide once and for all whether or not to advertise his possession of it. It was time to make up his mind.

He found himself frowning at the four men who were coming toward him along the line of shade. Two of them were carrying between them a large tool case, and one was pulling a small wagon which had other material on it. The group stopped fifty feet from Pendrake's plane. Then one of them came forward, fumbling in his pocket. He knocked on the cabin door.

'Something I'd like to ask you!' he yelled.

Pendrake hesitated, cursing silently. He had been assured that no one else had rented a plane hangar at this end of the field and that the big sheds nearby were empty, for use in future years only. Impatient, he activated the lever that opened the door. 'What——' he began. He stopped, choking a little. He stared at the revolver that glittered at him from a hand that was rock-steady, then glanced up at a face that—he saw with a start now—was covered by a flesh mask.

'Get out of there.'

As Pendrake climbed to the ground, the man backed warily out of arm's reach and the other men ran forward, pulling their wagon, carrying their tools. They stowed the stuff into the plane and climbed in. The man with the gun paused in the doorway, drew a package out of the breast pocket of his coat, and tossed it at Pendrake's feet.

'That'll pay you for the plane. And remember this: You will only make yourself look ridiculous if you pursue this matter further. This engine is in an experimental stage. We want to explore all its possibilities before we apply for a patent, and we don't intend to have simple secondary patents, improvements, and what not hindering our development of the invention. That's all.'

The plane began to move. Quickly, it lifted. It became a speck in the western sky and was merged into the blue haze of distance. The thought that came finally to Pendrake was: His decision had been made for him.

His sense of loss grew. So did his blank feeling of helplessness. For a while he watched the local planes taking off and landing on the northern runway; but after many minutes he was still without a plan or purpose.

He could go home. He pictured himself sneaking into his cottage in Crescentville like a whipped dog, with the long, long days still ahead of him. Or—the dark thought knit his brow—he could go to the police. The impulse jarred deeper and brought his first memory of the package that had been thrown at his feet. He stooped, picked it off the concrete, tore it open, and counted the green bills inside. When he had finished, he mustered a wry smile. A hundred dollars more than he had paid for the Puma.

But it was a forced sale and didn't count. With abrupt decision Pendrake started the engine of his borrowed truck and headed for the Dormantown station of the state police. His doubts returned with a rush as the police sergeant gravely noted down his charge.

'You found the engine, you say?' The policeman reached that point finally.

'Yes.'

'Did you report your find to the Crescentville branch of the state police?'

Pendrake hesitated. It was impossible to explain the instinctive way he had covered up his possession of the engine, without the engine as evidence of how unusual a find it was. He said at last: 'I thought at first it was a piece of junk. When I discovered it wasn't, I quickly learned that no such loss had been reported. I decided on the policy of finders keepers.'

'But the rightful owners now have it?'

'I would say so, yes,' Pendrake admitted. 'But their use of guns, their secrecy, the way they forced me to sell the plane convince me I ought to press the matter.'

The policeman made a note; then, 'Can you give me the manufacturer's number of the engine?'

Pendrake groaned. He went out finally into the brightening day, feeling that he had fired a dud shot into impenetrable night.

Three

He reached Washington by the morning plane from Dormantown and went at once to the office of Hoskins, Kendlon, Baker, and Hoskins, patent attorneys. A moment after his name had been sent in, a slim dandified young man broke out of a door and came loping across the ante-room. Oblivious of the startled amazement of the reception clerk, he cried out in a piercing voice:

'The Air Force's Man of Steel! Jim, I——'

He stopped. His blue eyes widened. Some of the color went out of his cheeks and he stared with a stricken look at Pendrake's empty sleeve. Silently he pulled Pendrake into his private office. He muttered, 'The man who pulled knobs off doors when he was in a hurry and crushed anything in his hands when he got excited——' He shook himself, threw off the gloom with an effort. 'How's Eleanor, Jim?'

Pendrake had known that the beginning was going to be hard. As briefly as possible, he explained: 'You know what she was like. She held that job in the research department of of the Hilliard Encyclopedia Company, an out-of-the-world existence that I pulled her away from, and——'

He stopped, shrugged finally, and went on: 'And then she found out somehow about those other women. I don't know who told her. She showed me a letter and asked me if it was true.'

Hoskins said gently, 'We were in Asia for three years. I had a dozen women while I was there; a couple of them were pretty good girls, too. I'd have married one of them if I hadn't already been married. What did the letter say, and who was it from?'

'I didn't read it,' said Pendrake. He sighed. 'I don't know why I fell for Eleanor. Must've reminded me of my mother or something. She had a power that made other women seem unimportant. But never mind that.'

Without preamble, he launched into a detailed account of the engine. By the time he reached the end of his story, Hoskins was pacing the office floor.

'A secret group with a new, marvelous engine invention.

Jim, this sounds big to me. I'm well connected with the Air Force and know Commissioner Blakeley. But there's no time to waste. Have you plenty of money?'

Pendrake was doubtful. 'It depends on what you mean by plenty.'

'I mean we can't waste time on red tape. Can you lay out five thousand dollars for the electron image camera? You know, the one that was invented just at the end of the war. Maybe you'll get your money back, maybe you won't. The important thing is that you go to that hillside where you found the engine and photograph the soil electrons. We must have a picture of that engine to convince the type of cynic that's beginning to show himself in town again, the fellow who won't believe anything he doesn't see, and gives you a sustained run-around if you can't show him.'

The man's energy and interest were contagious. Pendrake jumped up. 'I'll leave at once. Where can I get one of those cameras?'

'There's a firm in town that sells them to government and to various educational institutes for geologic and archaeologic purposes. Now look, Jim, I hate to rush you off like this. I'd like you to come home and meet my wife, but time is of the essence in those photographs. That soil is exposed to the light, and the image will be fuzzy.'

'I'll be seeing you,' Pendrake said, and started for the door.

The prints came out beautifully clear, the image of the machine unmistakable. Pendrake was sitting in his living room admiring the glossy finish when a messenger from the telephone office knocked.

'There's a long distance call for you from New York,' the messenger said. 'The party is waiting. Will you come to the exchange?'

'Hoskins,' Pendrake thought, though he couldn't imagine what Ned would be doing in New York. The first sound of the strange voice on the phone chilled him. 'Mr. Pendrake,' it said, 'we have reason to believe that you are still attached to your wife. It would be regrettable if anything should happen to her as a result of your meddling in something that does not concern you. Take heed.'

There was a click. The sharp little sound was still echoing in Pendrake's mind minutes later as he walked blankly along the street. Only one thing stood out clearly : The investigation was over.

The days dragged. Not for the first time it struck Pendrake that it was the engine that had galvanized him out of his long stupor. And that he had launched on the search as swiftly as he had because he had somehow realized that without the engine he would have nothing. It was worse than that. He tried to resume the old tenor of his existence. And he couldn't. The almost mindless rides on Dandy that once had lasted from dawn to dark ended abruptly, before 10 a.m. on two successive days, and were not resumed. It wasn't that he no longer wanted to go riding. It was simply that life was more than an idler's dream. The three-year sleep was over. On the fifth day a telegram arrived from Hoskins :

'WHAT'S THE MATTER ? I'VE BEEN EXPECTING TO HEAR FROM YOU.

NED'

Uneasily Pendrake tore the message to shreds. He intended to answer it, but he was still cudgeling his brain over the exact wording of his reply two days later when the letter arrived.

'. . . Cannot understand your silence. I have interested Air Commissioner Blakeley, and some technical staff officers have already called on me. In another week I'll look like a fool. You bought the camera; I checked on that. You must have the pictures, so for Pete's sake let me hear from you. . . .'

Pendrake answered that :

'I am dropping the case. I am sorry that I bothered you with it, but I have found out something that completely transforms my views on the affair, and I am not at liberty to reveal what it is.'

Wouldn't reveal it would have been the truth, but it

would be inexpedient to say so. These active Air Force officers—he had been one of them in his time—couldn't yet have gotten into their systems the fact that peace was radically different from war. The threat to Eleanor would merely make them impatient; her death or injury would constitute a casualty list so minor as to be beneath consideration. Naturally they would take precautions. But to hell with them.

On the third day after he sent the letter a taxi drew up before the gate of the cottage, and Hoskins and a bearded giant climbed out. Pendrake let them in, quietly acknowledged the introduction to the great Blakeley, and sat cold before his friend's questions. After ten minutes Hoskins was as white as a sheet.

'I can't understand it,' he raved. 'You took the photos, didn't you?'

No answer.

'How did they come out?'

Silence.

'This thing you learned that transformed your views—did you obtain further information as to who is behind the engine?'

Pendrake thought in anguish that he should have lied outright in his letter, instead of making a stupidly compromising statement. What he had said had been bound to arouse intense curiosity and this agony of interrogation.

'Let me talk to him, Hoskins.' Pendrake felt a distinct relief as Commissioner Blakeley spoke. It would be easier to deal with a stranger. He saw that Hoskins was shrugging as he seated himself on the sofa and nervously lighted a cigarette.

The big man began in a cool, deliberate tone: 'I think what we have here is a psychological case. Pendrake, do you remember that fellow who in 1956 or thereabouts claimed to have an engine that got its power from the air? When the reporters examined his car, they found a carefully concealed battery. And then,' the cold, biting voice went on, 'there was the woman who, two years ago, claimed to have seen a Russian submarine in Lake Ontario. Her story got wilder and wilder as the Navy's investigation progressed, and finally she admitted she had told the story to friends to arouse interest in herself, and when the publicity started she didn't have the nerve to tell the truth. Now, in your case, you're being smarter.'

The extent of the insult brought a twisted smile to Pendrake's face. He stood like that, staring at the floor, listening almost idly to the verbal humiliation to which he was being subjected. He felt so remote from the hammering voice that his surprise was momentarily immense as two large hands grabbed his lapels and the handsome bearded face pushed belligerently into his and the scathing voice blared:

'That's the truth, isn't it?'

He hadn't thought of himself as being wrought up. He had no sense of rage as, with an impatient sweep of his head, he broke the big man's double grip, whirled him around, caught him by the collar of his coat, and carried him, kicking and shouting in amazement, into the hallway and through the screen door onto the veranda. There was a wild moment as Blakeley was heaved to the lawn below. He came to his feet, bellowing. But Pendrake was already turning away. In the doorway he met Hoskins. Hoskins had his coat and bowler hat. He said in a level voice:

'I'm going to remind you of something——' He intoned the words of the pledge of loyalty to the United States. And he couldn't have known that he had won, because he walked down the steps without looking back. The waiting taxi was gone before Pendrake grasped how completely those final words had defeated his own purpose.

That night he wrote the letter to Eleanor. He followed it the next day at the hour he had named: 3.30 p.m. When the plump Negress opened the door of the big white house, Pendrake had the fleeting impression that he was going to be told that Eleanor was out. Instead, he was led through the familiar halls into the forty-foot living room. The venetian blinds were drawn against the sun, and so it took a moment for Pendrake to make out in the gloom the figure of the lithe young woman who had risen to meet him.

Her voice came, rich, familiar, questioning, out of the dimness: 'Your letter was not very explanatory. However, I had intended to see you anyway; but never mind that. What danger am I in?'

He could see her more clearly now. And for a moment he

could only stand there, drinking her in with his eyes—her slim body, every feature of her face, and the dark hair that crowned it. He grew aware that she was flushing under his intense scrutiny. Quickly he began his explanation.

'My intention,' he said, 'was to drop the whole affair. But just as I thought I had ended the matter by tossing Blakeley out, I was reminded by Hoskins of my Air Force oath to my country.'

'Oh!'

'For your own safety,' he went on, more decisive now, 'you must leave Crescentville for the time being, lose yourself in the vastness of New York until this matter has been probed to the bottom.'

'I see!' Her dark gaze was noncommittal. She looked oddly stiff, sitting in the chair she had chosen, as if she were not quite at ease. She said at last, 'The voices of the two men who spoke to you, the gunman and the man on the phone —what were they like?'

Pendrake considered. 'One was a young man's voice. The other, middle-aged.'

'No, I don't mean that. I mean the texture, the command of language, the degree of education.'

'Oh!' Pendrake stared at her. He said slowly, 'I hadn't thought of that. Very well educated, I should say.'

'English?'

'No. American.'

'That's what I meant. Nothing foreign, though?'

'Not the slightest.'

They were both, Pendrake realized, more at ease now. And he was delighted at the cool way she was facing her danger. After all, she wasn't trained to face down physical terrors. Before he could think further, she said :

'This engine—what kind is it? Have you any idea?'

Did he have any idea! He who had racked his brain into the dark watches of a dozen nights! 'It must,' said Pendrake carefully, 'have grown out of a tremendous background of research. Nothing so perfect could spring full-grown into existence without a mighty base of other men's work to build on. Though even with that, somebody must have had an inspiration of pure genius.' He added thoughtfully, 'It must be an atomic engine. It *can't* be anything else.

There's no other comparable background.'

She was staring at him, looking not quite sure of her next words. She said at last in a formal voice, 'You don't mind my asking these questions?'

He knew what *that* meant. She had suddenly become aware that she was thawing. He thought: 'Oh, damn these super-sensitive people!'

He said quickly, earnestly, 'You have already cleared up some important points. Just where they will lead is another matter. Can you suggest anything else?'

There was silence; then, 'I realize,' she said slowly, 'that I am not properly qualified. I have no scientific knowledge, but I do have my research training. I don't know whether my next question is foolish or not, but—what is the decisive date for an atomic engine?'

Pendrake frowned, said, 'I think I see what you mean. What is the latest date that an atomic engine couldn't have been developed?'

'Something like that,' she agreed. Her eyes were bright.

Pendrake was thoughtful. 'I've been reading up on it lately. Nineteen fifty-four might fit, but 1955 is more likely.'

'That seems like a long time—long enough.'

Pendrake nodded. He knew what she was going to say, and it was excellent, but he waited for her to say it.

She did after a moment. 'Is there any way you can check up on the activities of every able person who has done major atomic research in this country since that time?'

He inclined his head. 'I'll go first,' he said, 'to my old physics professor. He's one of those perpetually young old men who keep abreast of everything.'

Her voice, steady, cool, cut him off. 'You're going to pursue this search in person?'

She glanced involuntarily at his right sleeve as she finished, and then flushed scarlet. There was no doubt of the memory that was in her mind. Pendrake said swiftly, with a wan smile. 'I'm afraid there's no one else. As soon as I've made a little progress I'll go to Blakeley and apologize for treating him as I did. Until then, right arm or not, I doubt if there's anyone more capable than I am.' He frowned. 'Of course, there is the fact that a one-armed man is easily spotted.'

She had control of herself again. 'I was going to suggest that you obtain an artificial arm and a flesh mask. Those people must have worn civilian masks if you recognized the disguise so quickly. You can secure the perfect soldier type.'

She stood up and finished in a level voice : 'As for leaving Crescentville, I had already written my old firm, and they are hiring me in my former position. That was what I intended seeing you about. I shall leave the house tonight, and by tomorrow you should be free to pursue your investigations. Good luck.'

They faced each other, Pendrake shocked to the core by the abrupt termination of the meeting and by her words. They parted like two people who had been under enormous strain.

'And that,' Pendrake thought as he stood out in the sun's glare, 'is the truth.'

He remained in Crescentville that night. There were caretakers to hire, and among other things, Dandy to be returned to the stable at the big white house. It was nearly midnight when Pendrake took a bath preparatory to going to bed.

He lay back in the tub and loosened the bandage on the stump of his right arm. It had been uncomfortable, even painful for some days now. The bandage off, he started to lean over to soak the four-inch stump in the warm bath water.

He stopped.

And stared.

Then he let out a cry.

He subsided, trembling. And looked again. There was no doubt about it. The arm had grown in length a good two inches. And there was a faint outline of fingers and hand, tiny but unmistakable. They looked like a distortion of the smooth flesh.

It was nearly 3 a.m. before he could relax enough to sleep. By then, it seemed to him, he had reasoned out the only possible cause of the miracle. In all these exciting days, he had been near only one object that was different from all other objects in the world : the engine.

Now, indeed, he must find it. He had a strange thought about the ownership of the machine. Because of everything that had happened, because of the secrecy and the threats, and now this, it was as if he had progressively acquired rights. And so he had the distinct conviction, as he lay there in bed, that the great engine belonged to whoever could get hold of it.

Four

It was after midnight, October 8. Pendrake walked, head bent into a strong east wind along a well-lighted street in the Riverdale section of New York City. He peered at the numbers on the houses as he pressed by : 418, 420, 432.

Number 432 was the third house from the corner, and he walked on past it to the light post. Back to the wind, he stood in the bright glow, once more studying his precious list—a final verification. His original intention had been to investigate every one of the seventy-three eastern Americans on that list, starting with the A's. On second thought, he had realized that scientists of firms like Westinghouse, the Rockefeller Foundation, private laboratories with small means, and physicists and professors who were carrying on individual research were the least likely candidates, the former because of the impossibility of secrecy, the latter because that engine must have plenty of money behind it. Which left twenty-three private foundations.

Even that was a huge undertaking for one man; the chance of being caught put a strain on his face and into the muscles of his body and tightened up that growing arm. And this was only his eleventh investigation. The others had proved as fruitless as they were dangerous.

Pendrake put his list away and sighed. There was no use delaying. He had come down the alphabet to the Lambton Institute, whose distinguished executive physicist, Dr. McClintock Grayson, lived in the third house from the corner.

He reached the front door of the darkened residence and experienced his first disappointment. In a dim way, he had hoped the door would be unlocked. It wasn't, and that meant that all the doors he had opened in his life without ever noticing they were locked would now have to be precedents, proofs that a Yale lock could be broken silently. It seemed different, doing it on purpose, but he tensed himself and gripped the knob. The lock broke with the tiny click of metal that had been abruptly subjected to unbearable pressure.

In the inky hallway Pendrake stood for a moment, listening. But the only sound was the pounding of his heart. He went forward cautiously, using his flashlight as he peered into doors. Presently he verified that the study must be on the second floor. He took the stairs four at a time.

The hallway of the second floor was large, with five closed doors and two open ones leading from it. The first open door led to a bedroom, the second into a large, cozy room lined with bookshelves. Pendrake sighed with relief as he tiptoed into it. There was a desk in one corner, a small filing cabinet, and several floor lamps. After a swift survey, he closed the door behind him and turned on the trilight beside the chair next to the desk.

Once again he waited, listening with every nerve tensed. From somewhere came the faint sound of regular breathing. But that was all. The household of Dr. Grayson was resting peacefully from its day's labors, which—Pendrake reflected as he seated himself at the desk—was as it should be. He settled down to read.

At two o'clock he had his man. The proof was a scrawled note abstracted from a mass of irrelevant papers that cluttered one drawer. It read:

'The pure mechanics of the engine's operation depends on revolutions per minute. At very low r.p.m.—ie., fifty to one hundred—the pressure will be almost entirely on a line vertical to the axial plane. If weights have been accurately estimated, a machine will at this stage lift buoyantly, but the forward movement will be almost zero.'

Pendrake paused there, puzzled. It couldn't be anything but *the* engine that was being discussed. But what did it mean? He read on:

'As the number of r.p.m. increases, the pressure will shift rapidly toward the horizontal, until, at about five hundred revolutions, the pull will be along the axial plane—and all counter or secondary pressure will have ceased. It is at this stage that the engine can be pushed along a shaft, but not pulled. The field is so intense that——'

The reference to the shaft was ultimately convincing. He remembered only too well his own violent discovery that the shaft could not be pulled out of the engine.

The atomic wizard of the age was Dr. Grayson.

Quite suddenly Pendrake felt weak. He lay back in the chair, strangely dizzy. He thought: 'Got to get out of here. Now that I know, I absolutely mustn't be caught.'

The wild triumph came as the front door closed behind him. He walked down the street, his mind soaring with such a drunken exultancy that he swayed like an intoxicated person. He was eating breakfast at a lunch counter a mile away when the reaction came: So Dr. Grayson, famous *savant*, was the man behind the marvelous engine! So what now?

After he had slept, he called Hoskins long distance. 'It's impossible,' he thought as he waited for the call to be put through, 'that I carry on with this tremendous business all by myself.'

If anything should happen to him, what he had discovered would dissolve into the great darkness, perhaps never to be reconstituted. After all, he was here because he had taken to heart a timeless oath of allegiance to his country, an oath that he had not, until reminded, considered relevant.

His reverie ended as the operator said: 'Mr. Hoskins refuses to accept your call, sir.'

His problem seemed as old as his existence. As he sat in the hotel library that afternoon, his mind kept coming back to the aloneness of his position, the reality that all decisions about the engine were his to make and his to act upon. What an incredible fool he was! He ought to put the whole miserable business out of his mind and return to Crescentville. The property there would need attention before winter. But he knew he wouldn't go. What would he do in that lonely town during the long days and longer nights of the coming years?

There was only the engine. All his interest in life, his rebirth of spirit, dated from the moment that he had found the doughnut-shaped thing. Without the engine, or rather— he made the qualification consciously—without the search for the engine, he was a lost soul wandering aimlessly through the eternity that was *being* on Earth.

After a timeless period he grew aware suddenly of the weight of the book in his hands and remembered his purpose in coming to the library. The book was the 1968 edition of the Hilliard Encyclopedia, and it revealed that Dr. McClintock Grayson had been born in 1911, that he had one daughter and two sons, and that he had made notable contributions to the fission theory of atomic science. Of Cyrus Lambton the encyclopedia said:

'...manufacturer, philanthropist, he founded the Lambton Institute in 1952. Since the war, Mr. Lambton has become actively interested in a back-to-the-land movement, the uniquely designed headquarters for this project being located at...'

Pendrake went out finally into the warm October afternoon and bought a car. His days became a drab routine. Watch Grayson come out of his house in the morning, follow him until he disappeared into the Lambton Building, trail him home at night. It seemed an endless, purposeless game.

On the seventeenth day the routine finally broke. At one o'clock in the afternoon Grayson emerged briskly from the aerogel plastic structure that was the postwar abode of the Lambton Foundation.

The hour itself was unusual. But immediately the difference of this day from the others showed more clearly. The scientist ignored his gray sedan parked beside the building, walked half a block to a taxi stand, and was driven to a twin-turreted building on Fiftieth Street; a plasto-glitter sign splashed across the two towers:

CYRUS LAMBTON LAND
SETTLEMENT PROJECT

As Pendrake watched, Grayson dismissed the taxi and disappeared through a revolving door into one of the broad-based towers. Puzzled, but vaguely excited, Pendrake sauntered to a window that had a large illuminated sign on it. The sign read:

'THE CYRUS LAMBTON PROJECT wants earnest, sincere young couples who are willing to work hard to establish themselves on rich soil in a verdant and wonderful climate. Former farmers, sons of farmers and their daughters-of-farmers wives are especially welcome. No one who desires proximity to a city or who has relatives he must visit need apply. Here is a real opportunity under a private endowment plan.

'Three more couples wanted today for the latest allotment, which will leave shortly under the monitorship of Dr. McClintock Grayson. Office open until 11 p.m.

'HURRY!'

The sign seemed to have no connection to an engine lying on a hillside. But it brought a thought that wouldn't go away; a thought that was really a product of an urge that had been pressing at him for all the dreary days now past. For an hour he fought the impulse, then it grew too big for his willpower and projected down into his muscles, carried him unresisting to a phone booth. A minute later he was dialing the number of the Hilliard Encyclopedia Company.

There was a moment while she was being called to the phone. He thought a thousand thoughts, and twice he nearly hung up the receiver; and then, 'Jim, what's happened?'

The anxiety in her voice was the sweetest sound he had ever heard. Pendrake held himself steady as he explained what he wanted: 'You'll have to get yourself an old coat and put on a cheap cotton dress or something, and I'll buy some secondhand things. All I want is to find out what is behind the land-settlement scheme. We could go in before dark this evening. A simple inquiry shouldn't be dangerous.'

His mind was blurred with the possibility of seeing her again. And so the uneasy idea of possible danger stayed deep inside him and did not rise to the surface until he saw her coming along the street. She would have walked right past, but he stepped out and said:

'Eleanor!'

She stopped short; and, looking at her, it struck him for the first time that the slip of a girl he had married six years before was grown up. She was still slim enough to satisfy any woman, but the richer contours of maturity were there, too. She said, 'I forgot about the mask and the artificial arm. They make you look almost——'

Pendrake smiled tautly. She didn't know the half of it. His new arm was now almost elbow-length, and the hand and fingers were stubby and separated. The whole fitted firmly into the hollow tubing of the artificial arm and gave firmness and direction to its movements.

Intending to be humorous, for he was in an elated state, he said, 'Almost human, eh?'

He knew instantly that he had said the wrong thing. The color drained from her cheeks, then slowly crept back. She smiled wanly. 'I really don't mind your having only one arm. That was not our problem, though you tried to pretend that it was.'

He had forgotten. Now he remembered that in his emotional anguish at her rejection of him he had bitterly accused her of turning against him because he was not physically whole—it had been simply a verbal maneuver, but she had evidently been hurt by it.

She had turned away from him as he had these thoughts, and she was staring across at the building, a complacent smile on her lips. 'Aerogel turrets,' she mused aloud, 'a hundred and fifty feet high; one completely opaque windowless, doorless—I wonder what that means—and the other—— We'll be Mr. and Mrs. Lester Cranston of Winora, Idaho. And we were going to leave New York tonight but saw their sign. We'll love everything about their scheme.'

She started across the street. And Pendrake, tagging along behind, was following her through the door before, in one comprehensive leap of mind, he saw that it was his own emotional desire to see her that had impelled him to bring her here. 'Eleanor,' he said tensely, 'we're not going in.'

He should have known it would be useless to speak. She walked on, unheeding. He followed her with reluctant steps to a girl who sat at a spacious plastic desk in the center of the room. He was seated before the glitter sign at the edge of the desk caught his eye:

MISS GRAYSON

Miss Grayson! Pendrake twisted in his chair, and then a vast uneasiness held him steady. Dr. Grayson's daughter! So members of the scientist's family were mixed up in this. It was even possible that two of the four men who had taken the plane from him had been sons. And perhaps Lambton also had sons. He couldn't remember what the encyclopedia had said about the children of Lambton.

In the intensity of his thoughts he listened with half attention to the conversation between Eleanor and Grayson's daughter. But when Eleanor stood up, he remembered that the talk had been of a psychological test in the back room. Pendrake watched Eleanor walk across to the door that led to the second tower, and he was glad when, after about three minutes, Miss Grayson said:

'Will you go in now, Mr. Cranston?'

The door opened into a narrow corridor, and there was another door at the end of it. As his fingers touched the knob of the second door, a net fell over him and drew taught.

Simultaneously a slot opened to his right. Dr. Grayson, a syringe in his fingers, reached through, pushed the needle into Pendrake's left arm above the elbow, and then called over his shoulder to somebody out of sight:

'This is the last one, Peter. We can leave as soon as it gets dark.'

'Just a minute, Doctor. Better check that couple. Something funny about that guy's right arm. Look at this picture.'

The slot clicked shut.

Pendrake squirmed desperately. But he was becoming sleepy, and the net held him in spite of his writhing.

All in a flash, darkness descended.

Five

'In the two years since you've been here,' said Nypers, 'this firm has done very well.'

Pendrake laughed. 'You will have your joke, Nypers. What do you mean, in the two years since I've been here? Why, I've been here so long I feel like a graybeard.'

Nypers nodded his thin, wise head. 'I know how it is, sir. Everything else grows vague and unreal. There's a sense as if another personality has lived that past life.' He turned away. 'Well, I'll leave the Winthrop contract with you.'

Pendrake finally withdrew his astounded gaze from the impassive panels of the oak door beyond which the old clerk had vanished. He shook his head wonderingly, then in self-annoyance. But he grinned as he sat down at the desk.

Old Mr. Nypers must be feeling his oats this morning. 'In the two years since you——' Let's see now, how long *had* he been manager of the Nesbitt Company? Office boy at sixteen—that was in 1956—junior clerk at nineteen, then senior clerk, and finally manager. When the war came along in 1965 he had been given a leave of absence. Back at his desk in 1968, he had been hard at work ever since. Time blew by like a steady north wind.

Here it was 1975. H-m-m-m, sixteen years with the firm, not counting the war; seven as general manager. That made him exactly thirty-five years old this year.

He frowned, suddenly irritated. What could have motivated Nypers to say what he did? 'In the two years since you've been with us——' The words made a pattern in his mind. The action he took finally was semi-automatic. He pressed a button on his desk.

The door opened and a scrawny, white-faced woman of thirty-five or so came in.

'You rang, Mr. Pendrake?'

Pendrake hesitated. He was beginning to feel foolish and not a little amazed at his upset. 'Miss Pearson,' he said, 'how long have you been with the Nesbitt Company?'

The woman looked at him sharply, and Pendrake remembered too late that in these days of aggressive feminine emancipation an employer didn't ask a female employee questions that might be constructed as not being related to business.

After a moment Miss Pearson's eyes lost their hard, hostile gleam, and Pendrake breathed easier. 'Five years,' she said curtly.

'Who,' Pendrake forced himself to say, 'hired you?'

Miss Pearson shrugged, but the gesture must have been in connection with something in her own mind. Her voice was normal as she said, 'Why, the then manager, Mr. Letstone.'

'Oh,' said Pendrake.

He almost pointed out that he had been general manager for the past five years. He didn't, mainly because the thought behind the words skittered off into vagueness. His mind poised, blank, but relatively unconfused. The idea that finally came was logical and unblurred. He voiced it in a calm tone. 'Bring me the personnel accounts book for 1973, please.'

She brought the book and laid it on the desk. When she had gone out, Pendrake opened the volume at SALARIES for the month of December. And there it was: 'James Pendrake, general manager, $3250.'

November had the same story. Impatient, he thumbed back to January. It read:

'Angus Letstone, general manager, $2200.'

There was no explanation for the lower pay. February through August were all Angus Letstone, $2200.

Two years! 'In the two years since you've been with us——'

The Winthrop contract lay unread on the great oak desk. Pendrake stood up and went over and stared out of the vitreous glass windows that made a curving design at the corner of the room. A broad avenue spread below him, a tree-lined boulevard with many stone buildings. Money had flowed into this street—and into this room. He thought of how often he had believed himself one of those fortunate men at the lower end of the big-income class, a man who had attained the top position in his company after years of toil.

Ruefully Pendrake shook his head. The years of toil

hadn't occurred. The question therefore was, how had he got his excellent job with its pleasant salary, its exclusive clientele, its smoothly operating organization? Life had been as lovely and sweet as a drink of clear, cold water, an untroubled idyl, a simple design of happy living.

And now this!

How did a man find out what he had done during the first thirty-odd years of his life? There were a few simple facts that he could verify before taking any action. With abrupt decision, he returned to his desk, picked up his dictaphone, and began:

'Records Department, War Office, Washington, D.C. Dear Sir: Please send me as soon as possible my record for the Asian War. I was in the——'

He explained in detail, gathering confidence as he went along. His memory was so very clear on the main facts. The actual army life, the battles, were vague and far away. But that was understandable. There was that trip Anrella and he had taken to Canada last year. It was a dim dream now, with only here and there flashes of mental pictures to verify that it had ever happened.

All life was a process of forgetting the past.

His second letter he addressed to Birth Records Statistics in his home state. 'I was born,' he dictated, 'on June 1, 1940, in the town of Crescentville. Please send my birth certificate as soon as possible.'

He rang for Miss Pearson and gave her the dictaphone record when she came in. 'Verify those addresses,' he instructed briskly. 'I believe there's some small charge involved. Find out what, enclose money orders, and send both letters airmail.'

He felt pleased with himself. No use getting excited about this business. After all, here he was, solid in his job, his mind as steady as a rock. There was no reason to let himself become upset, and even less cause for allowing others to discover his predicament. In due course the answer to his two letters would arrive. Time enough then to pursue the matter further.

He picked up the Winthrop contract and began to read.

Twenty minutes later it struck him with a shock that he had spent most of the time striving to remember just what he had been doing during September 1973. In August there had been the internal squabble that had nearly split wide open the powerful union of women's clubs. And the headlines had been—what? Pendrake strained to remember, but nothing came. He thought, What about September 1? If August and September's beginning had been the dividing time, then September 1 should perhaps have some special quality of aliveness that would mark it distinctly. He had, he remembered vaguely, been sick about that time.

His mind wouldn't pin down that first day of the month of September. Presumably he had had breakfast. Presumably he had gone to the office after receiving one of Anrella's lingering good-by kisses. His mind poised in mid-flight like an animal that had been shot on the run. 'Anrella!' he thought. She must have been there on August 30 and 29, and in July, June, May, April, and back and back.

There was not in his whole memory the suggestion, nor had there been in her actions during the vital month of September, that they hadn't been married for years.

Therefore—*Anrella knew!*

It was a realization that had its emotional limitations. The curious dartings of his mind at the first sharp awareness of the idea were caught in the net of a quieter logic and grew calm. So Anrella knew. Well, so she ought. He had obviously been around for many years. Any change that had occurred had taken place in his mind, not in hers.

Pendrake glanced at the wall clock; a quarter of twelve. He'd just have time to drive home for lunch. He usually had lunch in town, but the information he wanted couldn't wait.

A number of good-looking women were standing in the hallway as he headed for the elevator. The impression that they stared at him sharply as he passed was so strong that Pendrake was torn out of his own tempestuous thoughts. He turned and glanced back.

One of the women was saying something into a little shining device on her wrist. Pendrake thought, interested: 'A magic jewel radio.'

He was in the elevator then, and he forgot the incident during the space of the downward trip. There were women in the lobby as he emerged from the elevator, and still others in the entranceway. At the curb stood half a dozen imposing black cars with a woman driver behind each steering wheel. In a few minutes the street would be swarming with the noon rush crowds. But now, except for the women, it was almost deserted.

'Mr. Pendrake?'

Pendrake turned. It was one of the young women who had been standing just outside the doorway, a brisk-looking woman with a strangely stern face.

Pendrake stared at her. 'Uh?' he said.

'You are Mr. James Pendrake?'

Pendrake emerged further out of his half reverie. 'Why, yes, I . . . What——'

'Okay, girls,' said the young woman.

Amazingly, guns appeared. They shone metallically in the sun. Before Pendrake could more than blink at them, hands caught at his arms and propelled him toward one of the limousines. He could have resisted. But he didn't. He had no sense of danger. In his brain was simply an enormous paralyzing astonishment. He was inside the car, and the machine was moving, before his mind resumed its functioning.

'Say, look here!' he began.

'Please do not ask questions, Mr. Pendrake.' It was the young woman who had already spoken to him; she sat now to his right. 'You are not going to be hurt—unless you misbehave.'

As if to illustrate the threat, the two women who sat on small pull-down center seats facing him with drawn guns wiggled their shiny weapons meaningfully.

After a minute it was still not a dream. Pendrake said, 'Where are you taking me?'

'Ask no questions, please!'

That brought impatience, a sense of being treated like a child. Grim, furious, Pendrake leaned back and with hostile eyes studied his captors. They were typical short-skirted 'new' women. The two armed women looked well over forty, yet they were slenderly, lithely built. Their eyes had the very bright look of women who had taken the Equalizer —Makes you the Equal of a Man—drug treatment. The young leader and the girl on Pendrake's left had the same bright-eyed appearance.

They all looked capable.

Before Pendrake could think further, the machine twisted around a corner and up a long, slanting incline of pavement. Pendrake had time to recognize that this was the garage entrance to the skyscraper McCandless Hotel, and then they were inside the garage and sweeping toward a distant door.

The car stopped. Without a word Pendrake obeyed the pistols that motioned him out. He was led along a deserted corridor to a freight elevator. The elevator halted at the third floor. Surrounded by his all-female guard, Pendrake was led slantwise across the gleaming corridor and through a door.

The room was large and lovely and magnificently furnished. At the far end, on a green lounge, his back to an enormous window, sat a fine-looking gray-haired man. To the man's right, at a desk, sat a young woman. Pendrake scarcely glanced at the latter. Wide-eyed, he watched as the youthful leader of his guards approached the gray-haired man and said:

'As you requested, President Dayles, we have brought you Mr. James Pendrake.'

It was the name, so blandly spoken, that confirmed the identification. Incredulous, he had already recognized the much-photographed face. There was no further room for doubt. Here was Jefferson Dayles, President of the United States.

Six

Anger gone, Pendrake stared at the great man. He was aware of the women who had escorted him leaving the room. Their departure pointed up the strangeness of this forced interview.

The man, he saw, was studying him narrowly. Pendrake noticed that, except for the gray eyes that glowed like ash-colored pearls, President Dayles looked his publicized age of fifty-nine. Newspaper photographs had suggested a youthful unlined face. But it was clear, gazing at him from this short distance, that the strain of this second campaign was taking its toll of the man's life force.

Nevertheless, the President's countenance was unmistakably strong, commanding, and handsome, with a serenity of assurance. His voice, when he spoke, had all the glowing, resonant power that had contributed so much to his great success. He said with the faintest of sardonic smiles, 'What do you think of my amazons?'

His laughter rolled homerically through the room. He obviously expected no answer, for his amusement ended abruptly and he went on without pause, 'A very curious manifestation, these woman. And, I think, a typically American manifestation at that. Once taken, the drug cannot be counteracted; and I regard it as an evidence of the basic will-to-adventure of American girls that some thousands took the treatment. Unfortunately, it brought them to a dead end, left them futureless. Unequalized women dislike them, and men think they're "queer," to use a colloquialism. Their existence may well have served the purpose of galvanizing the women's clubs into undertaking a presidential campaign. But as individuals, the amazons discovered that few employers would hire them and no man would marry them.

'In desperation their leaders approached me, and just before the situation reached the tragic stage, I arranged some skillful preliminary publicity and hired them en masse for what are generally believed to be perfectly legitimate purposes. Actually, these women know their benefactor and regard themselves as peculiarly my personal agents.'

Jefferson Dayles paused, then went on blandly, 'I hope, Mr. Pendrake, that this will explain to some extent the odd method by which you were brought before me. Miss Kay Whitewood'—he motioned to the young woman at the desk—'is their intellectual leader.'

Pendrake did not let his gaze follow the gesturing hand. He stood like a stone and was almost as blank mentally. He had listened to the brief history of the group of amazons with a fascinating sense of unreality. For the story explained nothing. It wasn't the means by which he had been brought here that counted. It was why.

He saw that the fine eyes were smiling at him in amusement. Jefferson Dayles said quietly. 'There is a possibility that you will wish to report what has happened to authorities or newspapers. Kay, give Mr. Pendrake the news item we have prepared to meet such an eventuality.'

The young woman rose from the chair at the desk and came around it toward Pendrake. Standing up, she looked older. She had blue eyes and a hard, pretty face. She handed Pendrake a sheet with typewritten lines on it. He read :

'Big Town, July 1975—An irritating incident disturbed President Jefferson Dayles's motor drive from Middle City. What seemed like an attempt to ram the President's car on the part of a young man in an electric automobile was frustrated by the prompt action of his guards. The young man was taken into custody and later brought to the presidential hotel suite for questioning. His explanations were considered satisfactory. Accordingly, at President Dayles's request, no charges were made, and the man was dismissed.'

After a moment Pendrake allowed himself a curt laugh. This doctored news item was, of course, final. He could no more engage in a newspaper duel with Jefferson Dayles than he could—well, ride up Main Street firing a six-shooter. Mentally he pictured the shouting headlines :

OBSCURE BUSINESSMAN ACCUSES
PRESIDENT DAYLES
Smear Campaign against the President

Pendrake laughed again, more sardonically this time. There seemed little doubt. Whatever Jefferson Dayles's reason for having him kidnaped—— His mind poised there. Whatever his reason! What could be his reason? Bewildered, he shook his head. He could contain himself no longer. His gaze fixed on the gray, half-amused eyes of the Chief Executive. 'All this,' he marveled, 'so much effort expended, such a dishonorable story deliberately prepared—for what?'

It seemed to him then, as he stared at the other, that the interview was about to get down to business.

The older man cleared his throat and said, 'Mr. Pendrake, can you name the major inventions originated since World War II?'

He stopped. Pendrake waited for him to go on. But the silence lengthened, and the President continued to look at him patiently. Pendrake was startled. It apparently was a genuine question, not just rhetoric. He shrugged and said, 'Well, there hasn't been much that is basic. I'm not up on these things, but I would say the rocket to the moon, and a few developments of the vacuum tube and——' He broke off blankly. 'But see here, what is all this? What——'

The firm voice caught at one of his sentences. 'There hasn't been much, you say. That statement, Mr. Pendrake, is the most tragic commentary imaginable on the state of our world. There hasn't been much. You mention rockets. Man, we don't dare tell the world that the rocket, except for minor details, was perfected during World War II and that it's taken us over thirty years to solve those minor details.'

He had leaned forward in the intensity of his argument. Now he sank back with a sigh. 'Mr. Pendrake, some people say that the cause of this incredible stagnation of the human mind is the direct result of the kind of world that came out of World War II. That, I think, is partly to blame. A bad moral atmosphere tires the mind in a curious, sustained fashion; it is hard to describe. It is as if the brain wears itself out fighting its intellectual environment.'

He paused and sat frowning, as if he were searching for a more definite description. Pendrake had time to think in amazement: Why was *he* being given this intimate, detailed argument?

The Executive looked up. He seemed to be unaware that

he had paused. He went on, 'But that is only part of the reason. You mentioned vacuum tubes!' He repeated is an oddly helpless voice, 'Vacuum tubes!' He smiled wearily. 'Mr. Pendrake, one of my degrees is an M.S., and that has made me aware of the tremendous problem confronting modern technology, the problem of the impossibility of one man learning all there is to know about even one science.

'But to get back to tubes—it is not generally known that for several years a number of famous laboratories have been picking up weak radio signals which are believed to originate on Venus. Six months ago I determined to find out why no progress was being made toward amplifying these signals. I invited three of the greatest men in their special electronic fields to explain to me what was wrong.

'One of these men designs tubes, another circuits; the third man tries to make the finished article out of the separate jobs of the other two. The trouble is, tubes are a lifetime study. The tube designer cannot but be hazy on circuits because that, too, is a lifetime study. The circuit man has to take what tubes he can get because, having only a theoretical knowledge of tubes, he cannot specify or even imagine what a tube should do in order to fulfill the purpose he has in mind. Among them, those three men have the knowledge to construct new and startlingly powerful radios. But over and over and over again they fail. They cannot conjoin their knowledge. They——'

He must have become aware of the expression on Pendrake's face. He stopped, and with a faint smile said, 'Are you following me, Mr. Pendrake?'

Pendrake bowed before the ironical twist in the other's smile. The long monologue had given him time to gather his thoughts. He said, 'The picture I'm visualizing is this: A small businessman has been forcibly picked up on the street and brought before the President of the United States. The President immediately launches into a lecture on radio and TV tubes. Sir, it doesn't make sense. What do you want from me?'

The answer came slowly. 'For one thing, I wanted to have a look at you. For another——' Jefferson Dayles paused, then: 'What is your blood type, Mr. Pendrake?'

'Why, I——' Pendrake caught himself and stared at the

man. 'My what?'

'I want a sample of your blood,' said the President. He turned to the girl. 'Kay,' he said, 'obtain the sample, please. I'm sure Mr. Pendrake will not resist.'

Pendrake didn't. He allowed his hand to be taken. The needle jabbed his thumb, bringing a faint stab of pain. He watched curiously as the red blood flowed up the narrow tube of the needle.

'That's all,' said the President. 'Good-by, Mr. Pendrake. It was pleasant meeting you. Kay, will you please call Mabel and have her return Mr. Pendrake to his office?'

Mabel was apparently the name of the leader of his escort, for it was she who came into the room, followed by the gun-women. In a minute Pendrake was out in the hall and in the elevator.

After Pendrake had gone, the great man sat with a fixed smile on his face. He looked over at the woman once, but she was staring down at her desk. Slowly Jefferson Dayles turned and gazed at a screen that stood in the corner near the window behind him. He said quietly, 'All right, Mr. Nypers, you may come out.'

Nypers must have been waiting for the signal. He appeared before the words were completed, and walked briskly to the chair the President indicated. Jefferson Dayles waited until the old man's fingers lay idly on the ornamental metal knobs of the chair arms, then said softly :

'Mr. Nypers, you swear that what you have told us is the truth?'

'Every word!' The old man spoke energetically. 'I have given you the history of our group without naming any names or places. We have reached an impasse where we may shortly need the help of the government, but until we ask it, I warn you—any attempt to investigate us may result in our refusing to give you our knowledge. I want that clearly understood.'

There was silence. Finally Kay said curtly, 'Do not threaten the President of the United States, Mr. Nypers.'

Nypers shrugged and continued, 'A little over two years ago Mr. Pendrake was accidently exposed to an unusual type of radiation. It was beyond our control to prevent such exposure. He found something we had lost, and then, instead of letting well enough alone, he traced us down, and so we learned that he—as some of us before him—had become toti-potent. During the more severe state, as regrowth progresses, the person with toti-potent cells loses his memory, and so we supplied Pendrake by sleep suggestion and hypnotic recordings with the memory we wanted him to have. As a toti-potent, he was returned to a youthful state, and his blood, properly transfused, can make youthful anyone of his blood type.'

'But such transfusions do not cause loss of memory in the person who receives them?' The woman, Kay, spoke the question quickly.

'Absolutely not!' said Nypers positively.

'How long,' asked President Dayles after a pause, 'will Mr. Pendrake remain in the toti-potent state?'

'He is in it all the time,' was the reply, 'but it is a latent condition until some body stress causes it to be activated. We have found that certain injections bring about such a condition of stress, though it takes several months for the cells to ripen to full toti-potency.'

'And these injections have now been given Mr. Pendrake?' the President said.

'Yes—by his doctor. Pendrake is under the impression that they are vitamin shots. We instilled in him an interest in such things, but he is normally an extremely healthy, virile, and active man. It's lucky for your girls that he didn't struggle.'

'They're as strong as men!' Kay snapped.

'They're not as strong as Jim Pendrake,' said Nypers. He seemed about to continue on that tack, then evidently thought better of it. He said instead, 'By late summer or early fall he will be approaching the extreme toti-potent state, and then you can be given a blood transfusion.' He addressed Jefferson Dayles, 'We keep a list of public figures of various blood types, and when yours was finally added to the list— this data is not always easy to obtain—we were overjoyed to discover that we had one person with a similar blood type: that is, under the classification AB, or Group IV by Jansky nomenclature. This put us in the position of being able to approach you with an offer that would enable us to accept your help without placing ourselves completely in your power.'

Kay said tartly, 'What is to prevent us from seizing and holding Mr. Pendrake until autumn?'

'The transfusion,' said Nypers firmly, 'requires special skill, and we have that skill. You don't. I hope that clarifies everything.'

Jefferson Dayles did not reply. His impulse was to close his eyes against brightness. But the brightness was in his brain, not outside it, and he had the shaky conviction that it could burn out his brain if he was not careful. At last he managed to turn to Kay. Relieved, he saw that she was looking up from the lie-detector register on her desk. The detector was connected to the ornamental knobs on the armchair in which Nypers sat. As he looked at her, Kay nodded slightly.

The brightness was abruptly like a white fire, and he had to fight to sit there, rigid, straining with his brain against the nameless joy that was swirling inside him. The desire came to rush over to Kay's desk and glare down at the detector face and compel Nypers to repeat his words. But that, also, he fought off. He grew aware that the old man was speaking again.

'Any further questions before I leave?' Nypers asked.

'Yes.' It was Kay. 'Mr. Nypers, you are not yourself a good example of toti-potent youthfulness. How do you explain this?'

The old man looked down at her with his bright eyes, which were the most alive part of his body. 'Madame, I have twice been rejuvenated, and now—frankly—I don't know. Shall I have it done again? The world is so grim, people so foolish, that I cannot decide to continue to remain alive in this primitive era.' He smiled faintly. 'My doctor tells me I am in good health, so I can still change my mind.'

He turned and walked to the door, paused there, facing them, his eyes questioning them. Kay said, 'This toti-potent phase of Pendrake—what is he like when he is in it?'

'That's his problem, not yours,' was the cool reply. 'But' —Nypers showed gleaming white teeth—'I would not be here if he were dangerous.'

With that, he departed.

When he had gone, Kay said savagely, 'That reassurance means exactly nothing. He's holding back vital information. What can their game be?' Her eyes narrowed with calculation. Several times she seemed on the verge of speaking but each time cut her words off by an odd trick of compressing her lips.

Jefferson Dayles watched the interplay of emotions on the intensely alive face, briefly absorbed by this curious woman who felt everything so violently. Finally he shook his head; his voice was strong as he said, 'Kay, it doesn't matter. Don't you see that? Their game, as you call it, means nothing. No one, no individual, no group, can stand up against the United States Army, Navy, and Air Force.' He drew a deep slow breath. 'Don't you realize, Kay, that the world is ours?'

Pendrake sat in a restaurant, eating. His attention was not on his food but on the two events of the morning. Each in turn struggled for his attention, gained it, then yielded to the other. Gradually the episode of Jefferson Dayles began to lose fascination. Because it meant nothing. It was like an accident happening to a man crossing a street, having no connection with the normal continuity of his life, and quickly forgotten once the shock and the pain were ended.

The rest, the problem of what had happened two years before, was different. It was still a part of his mind and of his body. It was of him, not to be dismissed by the casual assumption that somebody must be crazy. Pendrake glanced at his wrist watch. It showed ten minutes to one. He pushed away his dessert and stood up, determined to go at once and question Anrella.

His mind remained almost blank during the journey home. It was as he turned his automobile through the massive iron gates and saw the mansion that a new realization struck him. This house had been here, also, two years ago.

It was an amazingly expensive place, with an outdoor swimming pool and landscaped gardens, that he had got, according to his memory, at the bargain price of ninety thousand dollars. It had not occurred to him before to wonder how he had saved enough money to pay for such a splendid house. The sum had somehow seemed within his means.

The residence grew from the ground. The architect must have been an earnest disciple of Frank Lloyd Wright, for the skyline blended with the trees and land. There were sturdy chimneys, outjutting wings that merged coherently with the central structure, and a generous use of casement windows.

Anrella had always looked after the finances from their joint bank account. The arrangement left him free to devote his spare time to his lust for reading, his occasional golf, his fishing and hunting trips, his private airfield with its electric plane. And of course it left him free for his job. But it failed to provide him with any real idea of where he stood financially.

Again, and stronger now, he realized how odd it was that he had never worried or wondered about the arrangement. He parked the car and walked into the house, thinking, 'I'm a perfectly normal well-to-do businessman who's run up against something that doesn't quite fit. I'm sane. I have nothing to win or lose physically by any inquiry. My life is ahead of me and not behind me.' It wouldn't, he told himself earnestly, matter whether he ever learned anything or not. The past didn't count. He could live the rest of his life with scarcely more than a twinge of curiosity——— Where the devil was Nickson? Hat in hand, he stood in the great hallway waiting for the butler to acknowledge by his presence the sound of the door opening.

But no one came. Silence lay over the great house. He pressed buttons, but there was no answer. Pendrake tossed his hat onto a hall seat, peered into the deserted living room, and then headed for the kitchen.

'Sybil,' he began irritably, 'I want——'

He stopped. The reverberations of his voice echoed back at him from an empty kitchen. Nor were there any signs of the cook and the two pretty kitchen maids in the pantry or storeroom. A few minutes later Pendrake was climbing the main stairway when a sound of murmuring voices touched his ears.

The sound came from the upstairs drawing room. His hand on the knob, he paused when a spasmodic silence was broken by the clear voice of Anrella saying, 'Really, the argument is not necessary. At my age I have no feeling of possessiveness. You don't have to persuade me that poor Jim is the only logical person for the job. What have you done that you haven't told me?'

'We're bringing his wife back.' To Pendrake's amazement, it was the voice of Peter Yerd, one of the millionaire customers of the Nesbitt Company.

'Oh!'

'She should be in Crescentville in a couple of months or so.'

'What are you going to tell her?' Anrella's voice was steady.

'That isn't wholly decided, but if we deliver him to her about the time she returns, and she sees his condition and has the job of looking after him, she won't be any trouble.'

'That's true.' Anrella sounded thoughtful. 'What else have you done?'

Nypers' voice answered her, and momentarily that astounded Pendrake more than anything had so far. Then he thought, 'Of course.' What other explanation was there for what the old man had said to him than that he turn out to be one of the conspirators?

As Pendrake recovered from the shock, he was aware of Nypers describing the conversation of the morning. Nypers chuckled. 'I could see it working on him, and he later called for several files. So he started to think about it right there.'

The old man's dry voice continued, 'I find in myself an unsuspected gift for intrigue. I have done everything I was commissioned to do at our last meeting. Unsettling Mr. Pendrake was simple enough, but the interview with President Dayles involved, as we suspected, a careful phrasing of answers to counteract the lie detector. Since in all essentials I told the truth, I fear no repercussions, though I do believe that that woman will trace us. I'm afraid that's a risk we have to take.' He finished with quiet conviction, 'In my opinion, the time to inform the President was while he was here on the spot, able to meet Mr. Pendrake face to face.'

'We really have no alternative,' said a new voice—and Pendrake felt staggered once more, for it was the voice of Nesbitt himself, owner of the Nesbitt Company. 'We're being threatened with annihilation. The murders were carried out as if someone understood the entire Lambton project. If we're right—if the East Germans, acting under Soviet direction, are responsible—then it's no longer a matter for private action alone. We need help. The government has to be called in. Hence, this preliminary approach to President Dayles.'

The voice of Nickson, the butler, said firmly, 'Still, what we're doing adds up to one last private effort.'

As Pendrake strove to grasp that even the servants were leading figures in the group, Sybil, the maid, said with quiet authority, 'Anrella, we're even considering sending Jim to the moon.'

'Whatever for?' Anrella seemed genuinely surprised.

Sybil answered, 'My dear, we're coming to a severe emergency, and it's time we checked the late Mr. Lambton's story about where the engine came from.'

'Well,' said Anrella after a pause, 'Jim is certainly the logical person to go, since he's the only one who couldn't give away our secrets if anything went wrong.' She sounded resigned.

Afterward Pendrake cursed himself for leaving at that point. But he couldn't help it. Fear came, the fear that he would be discovered here, now, before he could think about what he had heard. He slipped down the stairs, snatched his hat and headed for the door. As he emerged into the open, he saw for the first time that nearly a dozen cars were parked on the far side of the house. He'd been too intent to notice them when he came in.

A few minutes later he was guiding his own machine through the iron gates and along the old farmer's road to the city highway. He had a strong conviction that it was going to be an afternoon of mental turmoil.

Eight

The days ran their swift course, and life went on. Every morning, except Saturday and Sunday, Pendrake climbed into his car and drove to work. Every evening he drove back again to the great house inside the iron fence to an evening meal that was served amid impeccable surroundings by highly trained servants, to a pleasant, relaxed period of reading in his study, and finally to the bed that he shared with a beautiful and loving woman.

The events that had disturbed him so much began to seem just a little unreal. But he did not forget them, and he consciously thought of himself as a man who was biding his time.

On the seventeenth morning, the letter arrived with his birth certificate. Pendrake read it with satisfaction and, he admitted it frankly to himself, relief.

There it was in black and white : James Somers Pendrake. Born June 1, 1940, town of Crescentville, County of Goose Lake. Father : John Laidlaw Pendrake. Mother : Grace Rosemary Somers——'

He had been born. His memory had not played him false. The world was not completely upside down. There was a gap in his memory, not an abyss. His position had been that of someone balancing on one foot beside a chasm of immeasurable immensity. Now he was like a man straddling a narrow though deep pit. It was true that the pit had to be filled in, but even if it wasn't, he could walk on without the horrible sensation of tottering in pitch-darkness on the edge of a cliff.

A sharp weakness seized Pendrake as he sat there. He swayed, recovered himself, then lay back heavily against the back of the chair. The astounded thought came : 'Why, I'm on the point of fainting.'

The nausea went away. Carefully Pendrake climbed to his feet and filled a glass with water. Back in his chair, he raised the glass to his lips—and saw that his hand was trembling. It startled him. He had, he realized, really let his situation affect him. Thank God, the worst of the purely personal part was over; not entirely over, it was true. But at least he had his beginning established. As soon as his military record arrived he'd be solidly based up to the age of twenty-four. It was a pretty sound base, if you really thought it over. And his conscious life had resumed at the age of thirty-three; that left nine years to be accounted for.

The high confidence drained. Nine years! It was not exactly a short time. In fact, it was damn long.

His military record arrived on the afternoon of the nineteenth. It was a printed form, on which the answers were typed in blank spaces provided.

There was his name, his age ... Air Force unit ... the name of his next of kin, 'Eleanor Pendrake, wife.' Serious wounds or injuries: 'Amputation of right arm below shoulder necessitated by injury in fighter plane crash——'

Pendrake stared. But he still had his right arm, he thought with owl-like gravity.

The gravity broke as he stared at the unchanging printed form. At last he thought: 'What a mistake. Some fool up in the records office has typed the wrong information.' Even as one part of his brain developed that argument, another part accepted everything, accepted and knew that there was no mistake, that there was nothing wrong with this form. The wrongness, the mistake, was not out there in some government department. It was here, in him. But there was no fooling anymore. Obviously, he was not the Jim Pendrake described in these records.

The time had come, therefore, to confront those who knew who he was. Whatever their purpose in impressing upon him the belief that he was Jim Pendrake, it must now be forced out into the open.

It was four o'clock as he turned through the open, twenty-foot-high gate and guided his car along the driveway, which wound scenically in and out among the trees. He drove the machine into the huge garage. Anrella's chauffeur, who acted as general mechanic around the estate, came over.

Gregory said, 'Home early, Mr Pendrake?'

'Yes!' said Pendrake in the deliberate tone of a determined man.

As he walked across the garden toward the french windows, a shadow glided over the ground past him. He looked up and saw that it was of a plane that was coming toward his private landing field. In rapid order four more planes followed the first one, and all of them disappeared behind the trees.

Pendrake was frowning over the intrusion, when Anrella came to the window. She called, 'What was that, dear?'

He told her, and she said, startled, 'Planes!' Instantly she added, 'Jim—get into your car! Leave at once!'

He stared at her. 'You'd better come too.'

She came running, which was a strange sight in itself. As she climbed into the car, she urged him breathlessly, 'Jim—if you value your freedom—*hurry*!'

As his car hurtled toward the gate that led to Alcina, Pendrake saw two Jeeps drive into the gateway and block his way. He slowed and since he would have to turn around to get away, stopped. One of the Jeeps roared over.

The cool-eyed women who operated it pointed the steadiest pistols Pendrake had ever faced. They motioned him to go back to the house. He did so without a word, but he had already recognized that these were the special women agents of President Dayles, and it relieved him slightly.

At the house he saw that the whole gang had been rounded up. Gathered in the garden were Nesbitt, Yerd, Shore, Cathcott, and all the servants including Gregory; altogether, nearly forty people were lined up before a regular arsenal of machine guns manned by about a hundred women.

'That was he all right!' reported the leader of the Jeep crew that had captured him. 'You were right in thinking they might try to get him away quickly.'

The woman she reported to was young and good-looking but very serious of face. She nodded curtly and ordered now in a deep voice, 'Put a guard on Jim Pendrake night and day. Only his wife can be permitted with him. All the others will be removed by plane to Kaggat Prison. Action!'

A few minutes later Pendrake was alone with Anrella. 'Darling,' he asked tensely, 'what is all this about?' It seemed to him that now at last the information could no longer be denied to him.

She had been standing at the window of the great living room, gazing out. Now she turned and came toward him and put her arms around him. She kissed him lightly on the lips. Then she leaned back and shook her head. There was a faintly humorous smile on her face.

A fury of reaction exploded in Pendrake's brain. He was dimly aware as he pulled away from her embrace that the swiftness of his anger showed how raw his nerves had worn during these weeks. 'You've got to tell me!' he raged. 'How can I even think unless I know more? Don't you see, Anrella——'

He stopped. The same amused expression was on her face. Some of his anger faded, but he was stiff and feeling vaguely insulted when he spoke again. 'I suppose you know,' he said, 'that no one but Jefferson Dayles could have sent these women thugs. If you do know that, and know why, tell me so that I can start figuring a way out.'

'There's nothing to figure out,' she said. 'We might as well stay here in confinement as anywhere.'

Pendrake stared at her. 'Are you crazy?' he said. Suddenly he felt completely out of his depth. He shouted, 'I overheard you at that meeting that day.'

Her face changed. The smile faded. 'What meeting?' she asked sharply.

When he told her, she looked concerned. 'What did you hear?'

'You said something about a change being due. What did that mean? A change in what?'

Her expression changed again. The concern was gone. 'I guess you didn't hear too much. The change is in you. That's all I'll tell you.'

He waved a hand at her, as if he were groping through darkness. 'You've told me this much. Why not tell me more?'

She was amused again. 'I haven't told you anything,' she said. She came to him and put her arms around him again and gazed up at him with eyes that were intelligent and wise and gentle and smiling. She said, 'Jim, the change comes more quickly when you're under strain, and you are, aren't you?' She broke off. 'It's been fun for you, hasn't it, Jim? Two years of unadulterated pleasure.'

He was too angry to consider the truth of that. He snapped, 'According to what I heard, you're not even my wife.'

'So we provided you with a woman companion,' she said. 'You'll have to admit it was all free. In fact, you've been well paid.'

In his frame of mind, that sounded like the final insult. 'I'm not the gigolo type,' he said harshly, whirled, and left the room.

He felt completely through with her.

That night, after they had gone to bed, Anrella said, 'We may be here for months. Are you going to be unfriendly during the whole time?'

Pendrake turned over and looked at her where she lay in the other twin bed. He said sharply, 'Months?' He felt baffled. Presumably there was a moment when the imprisonment would end—for a reason that she knew. He calmed himself with an effort. 'You're not going to tell me a thing?' he asked.

'No.'

'But you'd like to play house the whole time?'

'As always. '

He shook his head, but he could not quite bring himself to be angry, and so it was not entirely a rejection. 'I'll think it over,' he said slowly, 'but maybe you know that a man is not constructed just to sit still in such a situation as this. At least I'm not.'

'You do as you feel about that,' was her reply, 'but don't be unfriendly.'

He stared at her unhappily. 'If I give in to that thought,' he said, 'I'll become just another lotus eater. I could easily dream away the days and weeks in a sexual idyl.'

'That's not the worst thing that could ever happen.' She laughed softly. 'Is it?'

'There speaks the lotus,' he said. 'What about my real wife?'

A touch of color came into her cheeks. When she spoke, it was in a slightly defensive tone. 'I didn't make up my mind to undertake this relationship until after we established that she and you hadn't been living together for years.' She added, 'I believe your wife had decided to permit the marriage to resume, but that hadn't happened yet.'

Pendrake, who had asked his question halfheartedly—that . . . other life . . . was unreal—looked over at Anrella again.

She was back to her lighthearted state, for she smiled again.

The summer drifted dreamily by. As he had expected, he became restless. But it was not till the first hint of autumn began to show that Pendrake finally determined that it was time to wake up.

Nine

Pendrake fingered the rock. He strove so hard for casualness that his hand shook. He grew alarmed, fearful that he might give himself away. He settled closer to the velvet-like grass on which he sprawled, surrounded by his seven women guards.

The rock was two inches in diameter, two inches of inert stone. Yet it contained in its tiny mass so much of his hope that he trembled in a brief funk. Gradually, however, he quieted down and settled himself to wait for the boys. Every Saturday since school had started at the beginning of September he had heard their shrill voices at this time of the day. The sound came from beyond a fringe of trees that hid from his gaze the iron fence which completely surrounded the estate that had become his personal penitentiary.

The trees and fence separated them from him, and him from all the world. He hadn't dreamed that escape would take so much planning, such an intricate scheme, and two long months of otherwise uneventful waiting. During those months he'd stopped wondering why no one came from the office to inquire about him; undoubtedly someone else must be running the firm. He'd completely given up trying to be serious with Anrella. She wouldn't have it.

It was a bad situation. In minutes now the boys would be going past with their fishing rods, heading toward the deep pools farther upstream. And he had no plan to rely on but his own—— What was that?

It was, he realized tensely, a sound, a faint vibration of boyish laughter, far away as yet.

But the time had come.

Pendrake lay still, tautly examining his chances. Two of the women lolled at ease on the ground a dozen feet to his right. Three other women lounged eight feet to his left, and somewhat behind him.

He had no inclination to underestimate them. He did not doubt that he had been assigned guards strong enough to handle their weight in ordinary men. Of the two remaining women, one stood directly behind him at a distance of perhaps eight feet. The other loomed about six feet ahead, directly between him and the tall trees that hid the fence beyond which the boys would be passing. The smoky gray eyes of this powerful creature looked dull and unalert, as if her mind were far away. Pendrake knew better than that. She was a Jefferson Dayles machine, and she was the most dangerous thing on his horizon.

The medley of sound that preceded the boys was nearer. Pendrake felt the throb in his temples as he reached with a forced deliberateness into his pocket and slowly drew out a glass crystal. He held the little thing in his fingers, letting the rays of the morning sun lance its depths with fire. It blazed as he spun it into the air. As he caught it, snuffing its brilliant light, he was preternaturally conscious of eyes on him, the guards watching him, not with suspicion, but with awareness. Three times Pendrake flung the glass up several yards into the sky. And then, as if abruptly tiring of the game, he threw it to the ground about an arm's length from him. The crystal lay there, glittering in the sun, the brightest object in his vicinity.

He had given much thought to that glass crystal. It was obvious that no one of the guards could ever maintain a concentrated watch on him. Of the seven, he must assume that three were glancing at him with attention at one moment. When he finally moved, even these would have to look twice, because the reflected flame of the crystal would confuse their gaze and distort their mental pictures of what he was actually doing.

That was the theory—and the boys were nearer.

Their voices rose and fell, a happy babble, now boastful, now in agreement, now one dominating, now all speaking at once. It was impossible even to begin guessing how many there were. But they were there, physical realities, the presences he needed for his plan of escape.

Pendrake drew the book out of his left coat pocket. He opened it idly, not at the place marked, but glancing here and there, wasting time, anything to give the women the necessary seconds to adjust their minds to the immensely normal fact that he was going to read. He waited a moment longer. And then—he put the book down on the grass with its top edge pressed against the rock.

He opened the book boldly now at the marker, which was a sheet of notepaper. To the guards, the letter must look exactly like the scores of pieces of blank paper he had used in the past two months for taking notes. What was more, it was blank.

In spite of his determination to end an intolerable confinement, he actually had nothing to say to any local authorities. Until he knew what was involved in the whole wretched business, the problem was his. Once outside, he could handle it in his own way. He felt quite capable.

There was a stirring to his right. Pendrake did not look up, but his heart sank. The two women from whom he expected minimum interference were beginning to show life. What damnable luck!

But there could be no delay now. His fingers touched the white missive; perspiring, he shoved it out over the edge of the book and directly on top of the rock. The sheet, with all its carefully attached elastics, which needed only to be slipped over the little rock to clutch at it with dozens of tiny rubber strands, was quickly attached.

With a yell—to startle the women—he lurched to his feet and, with all his strength, flung the stone and its white, fluttering cargo.

He had no time to recover his balance to protect himself. Two bodies struck him simultaneously from different angles, flung him ten feet. Pendrake lay where he fell, dizzy from the blow, but conscious that he wasn't hurt. He heard the leader, the big woman who had been standing in front of him, snapping commands : 'Carlo, Marian, Jane—back to the house—get Jeeps—cut those kids off from town. Quick, Rhoda! Head for the gate, open it for them. Nancy, you and I will climb that fence and chase after the boys or hunt for that letter. Olive, you stay here with Mr. Pendrake.'

Pendrake heard the sound of footsteps as the guards raced off. He waited. Give them time. Give Nancy and the leader opportunity to get over the fence. And then—step two.

At the end of two minutes he began to groan. He sat up. He saw that the woman was watching him. Olive was a handsome though rather big-boned woman with a thin mouth. She came over.

'Need any help, Mr. Pendrake?'

Mister Pendrake! These people with their polite solici-
tude were driving him crazy. He was being illegally restrained. Yet it was all done with tenderness. But if he was
ever going to escape, it had to be now. The trick of getting
rid of his guards would not be repeatable. Pendrake made a
struggle of climbing to one knee. Then knelt, shaking his
head as if he were still dazed. He muttered finally, 'Give me
a hand.'

He didn't quite count on the woman actually assisting
him, although even that was possible in view of everyone's
helpful attitude.

But she did. She came over and started to bend down.
That was when Pendrake started up. There was no mercy in
him in that moment as he struck. These woman, with their
guns and their ruthlessness, were asking for trouble. A
lightning one-two, one-two to the jaw ended the engage-
ment in the first round.

Olive went down like a log. With utter abandon, exactly
as if he were attacking a man, Pendrake plunged on top of
her and rolled her over. Swiftly he drew from his pocket
one of the gags he had prepared. It took about a minute to
tie it over her mouth.

In a more leisurely fashion now, but without wasted
effort, Pendrake pulled out his shirttails and began to un-
wind the tough clothesline from his waist. As the woman
squirmed weakly, he started his tying-up job.

It required a little over three minutes. He stood up then,
shaky but calm. He wasted no further glance on his
prisoner, but strode off, keeping for a while parallel to the
fence. He pushed through the trees finally, scrutinized the
territory beyond the fence, and it was as he remembered it :
thickly wooded. Satisfied, Pendrake approached the fence
and began to climb it. As he had discovered in his first
attempt more than two months before, the fence itself was
not hard to climb. It was almost like shinnying up a rope.

He reached the top, eager now, and hitched himself over
the spear points of the fence. Afterward he realized that he
had become too eager.

He slipped.

He made a second mistake then : the instinctive mistake
of trying blindly to save himself. As he fell, one of the spears

jabbed into his right forearm, just below the elbow, and went through. He hung there, his arm skewered to that meathook of a fence. The pain crashed and roared through his body, and something warm and salty and viscid spurted against his mouth and into his eyes, a choking, blinding horror.

For seconds there was nothing else.

He was lifting himself. That was the first thing Pendrake knew over and above the tearing agony. Lifting himself with his left arm and simultaneously trying to raise his right forearm clear of the dark, clumsy spear that had transfixed it.

Lifting! And succeeding! Succeeding! Gibbering, he fell twenty feet to the ground below.

He struck hard. The muscles of his body were pain-clenched cords without give in them. The blow of landing was a bone-jolting smash from the sixty-six-million-million-billion-ton battering-ram that was Earth. He sank down, then got up again like an animal, with only one impulse left in his shattered body. Get away! Get out of here! They'd be coming, searching. Get out! Get out!

No other consciousness touched Pendrake until he reached the stream. The water was warm, but it was an autumn warmth. It soothed his burning lips: it brought sanity back to his feverish eyes. He washed his face, then struggled out of the sleeve of his coat and soaked and washed his arm. The water turned red. The blood welled and bubbled from a wound so gaping and terrible that he swayed and just in time flung himself backward onto the grassy bank.

How long he lay there, he had no idea. But he thought finally, 'Tourniquet, or die!' With an effort of will as much as of strength, he tore the damp and bloody shirt sleeve at the shoulder and wound it around and around the upper part of his arm. He twisted it tight with the short, broken end of a tree branch, twisted it so tight that it hurt his muscles. The bleeding stopped.

He staggered to his feet and began to follow the stream. That had been his original intention, and now his body remembered. It was easier to follow a previously chosen route than to think out a new one. Time passed. Just when the idea came that it wouldn't do to go straight to the savings bank, he couldn't have told afterward. But somewhere on the journey he met somebody and said:

'Hurt my arm! Where does the nearest doctor live?'

There must have been an answer. Because after another lapse of inestimable time he was walking along a street thinly overhung with autumn foliage. He realized at intervals that he was looking for a plaque with a name on it. All feeling had long since gone from his arm. It hung down, swinging as he walked, but it was the lifeless sway of an inanimate object.

He grew weaker, and weariness lay on him like a weight. He kept touching the tourniquet to make sure it wasn't loosening and permitting the blood that still remained to him to seep out. Then he was climbing steps on his knees.

'Christmas!' a man's voice said. 'What's this?'

There was a gap, through which a voice penetrated at intervals; then he was in an automobile, with that same voice waxing and waning in his ears.

'You incredible fool, whoever you are. You've had that tourniquet on an hour at least. Didn't you know—tourniquets must be loosened every fifteen minutes—to let the blood flow—arm must have blood to stay alive. Nothing now but to amputate it!'

Pendrake awakened suddenly and, turning his head, stared dully at the stump of his arm. His whole shoulder was raised on a kind of netted sling, and the arm was bare and plainly visible. An infra-red lamp poured heat on it, and the remnant felt cozy and comfortable and not at all painful.

It was not bleeding, and there was growth from it, a curled, pink, fleshy thing that seemed like some torn part of the shattered arm, which for some reason had not been cut off. Then he saw that it had a shape.

He stared and stared, and there was a memory in him of a military record that had read: 'Amputation of arm necessitated by——'

He slept, even as he tried to solve the puzzle.

Far away a man's voice was saying, 'There's no longer any doubt. It's a new arm growing in place of the torn-off one. We've been doing a little surgical work—though, as I said to Pentry, I'm hanged if I don't believe the growth is basically so healthy that it could get along without medical attention. It'll be several days before he regains full consciousness. Shock, you know.'

The voice faded, then came back:

'Toti-potent ... toti-potent cells. We've always known, of course, that every human cell has latent in it the form of the whole body; somewhere in the remote past the body apparently took the easier course of simply repairing damaged tissues.'

There was a pause. Pendrake had the distinct impression that someone was rubbing his hands together in satisfaction. A second man's voice murmured something inaudibly, then the first voice went resonantly on, 'No clues yet to his identity. Dr. Philipson, who brought him here, never saw him before. Of course a lot of people from both Big Town and Middle City live all through the Alcina district but ... No, we're not giving out any publicity. We want to watch further developments in that arm first. Yes, I'll phone you.'

The murmuring, second voice said something, and then there was the sound of a door closing.

Sleep came like a soothing blanket of forgetfulness.

When he awakened next, he didn't know who he was.

Realization of this came when a nurse, noticing he was awake, called the doctor. The doctor came in, followed by a second nurse, notebook in hand. The doctor sat down happily and said in a cheerful tone, 'And now, sir, what is your name?'

The man on the bed stared at him, puzzled. 'My what?'

Some of the high excitement went out of the other man. His voice was already subdued as he said slowly, 'What are you called? You know—your name?'

The nameless being on the bed lay very quiet. He had no difficulty grasping the concept. Without thinking how he understood it, he realized that this was Dr. James Trevor and that this was what a name was. Finally he shook his head.

'Try!' the man urged. 'Try to remember!'

A trickle of sweat sagged down Pendrake's face. All through his lean, strong body he felt the gathering tension of enormous effort, and there was a sudden sharp pain in his arm. In the vaguest way, he was aware of the white-starched figure of his nurse, and of the other nurse sitting with pencil poised over a notebook, and of the dark night beyond the window.

He gritted the pain out of his mind and, with the whole strength of that mind, strained to penetrate the mesh of waver and blur that lay like a cloud over his memory. Pictures took vague shape there, formless thoughts and shadow memories of days unutterably dim. It was not memory, but memory of memory. He was isolated in a little island of impressions of the moment, and the terrible sea of blankness all around was sweeping closer, pushing harder every minute, every second.

With a gasp he let the pressure of effort and strain slacken inside him. He stared helplessly at the doctor.

'Useless,' he said simply. 'There's something about an iron fence and—— What city is this? Maybe that will help.'

'Middle City,' the doctor said. His brown eyes watched Pendrake narrowly. But the latter shook his head.

'What about Big Town?' the doctor asked. 'That's a city about forty miles from here. Dr. Philipson brought you to Middle City from Alcina because he knows the hospitals here.' He repeated slowly, 'Big Town!'

For a moment there seemed to be a fuzzy familiarity. And then Pendrake shook his head. He stopped the weary movement as an idea struck him. 'Doctor, how is it that I can use the language, when everything else is so dim?'

The doctor stared at him, unsmiling, grim. 'You won't be able to speak in a few days unless you spend every possible minute reading and talking just to keep those particular conditioned reflexes alive.'

He was aware of the doctor half turning from him, facing the two nurses. 'I want a detailed, typewritten account prepared for the patient, giving the complete story of his case as far as we know it. Have a radio brought in here, and'— he turned back to the bed, smiling darkly—'you keep it on. Listen to the soap operas, if no one else is talking. When you're not listening or sleeping, read, read aloud.'

'What if I don't?' His lips were ash-dry. 'Why do I have to do this?'

The doctor's voice was grave. 'Because, if you don't, your brain will become almost as blank as a newborn baby's. There may be'—he hesitated—'other reactions, but we don't know what. We do know that you are forgetting your past at an alarming rate. We're reasoning that ordinarily the cells in the human body and brain are in a continuous state of being used and being repaired. Every hour, every day, our billions of memory cells are undergoing that repair; and apparently, in the mending, the little wave of memory electrically stored away is not damaged. In the long run, no doubt, the replacement of tissue diminishes the memory. Now, with you, it's different. You have at this instant toti-potent cells. Instead of being repaired, your arm cells have been replaced by brand new, healthy cells; and those new cells know nothing of the memory carried by the old, for memory, apparently, is not hereditary. If they do remember, the mechanism for transmitting that memory is not available. Therefore, you have cells as potentially capable of storing memory as your old ones, but all you can store in them before they in turn are replaced will be the impressions gained by your mind in a period of, say, a week, perhaps a little longer. Apparently the process of toti-potency, once it began in your arm, has spread to your body. The completeness of it is a little surprising, because laboratory tests of planarian worms have established that conditioned reflexes carry over into the new growth. We may surmise that memories will leave some trace behind. But words and simple, learned actions evidently fade below the level of usefulness.'

'But what am I going to do in the future?' Pendrake asked in bewilderment.

'We've sent your fingerprints to Washington,' the doctor said soothingly. 'Once your identity is established, we can work out a continuous, re-educational program based on the truth. Meanwhile, do as I've suggested.'

Pendrake stared at the man, and as he studied him a feeling came through of excitement, and interest, and some sympathy. 'But he's more interested in the phenomenon than in the man,' Pendrake thought.

He also had a feeling from inside his body that the situation was not so bad as the doctor anticipated and that, once the new growth was completed, a condition of normalcy would be established.

Eleven

The new man said, 'I'm Dr. Coro, Mr. Smith. I'm a psychologist, and I would like to give you some tests. Is that all right?'

The almost nameless man on the bed stared at the newcomer with bright eyes. He recognized that he was being treated like a child, which did not disturb him. And he divined, in a way he had of knowing, that most of the tests would not be workable with him—just why was not clear—nor did it occur to him to wonder how he knew it.

But he said nothing, simply watched as the psychologist, taking consent for granted, spread some papers out on the bedside table, pulled up a chair, and sat down. He was a sturdily built man, with a firm, kindly manner, and he explained patiently that he had talked with 'your doctor, and he thinks it would be good for all of us to know what's going on in your brain. Is that all right?'

Again Pendrake said nothing. The miasma of thought and feeling that came from Dr. Coro did not actually permit any answer except yes. Pendrake was not resistant, so he simply waited.

Dr. Coro placed one of his sheets on a clipboard and handed the board and a pencil to Pendrake. 'That is a maze,' he said. 'Now, I want you to take the pencil, place the point at the arrow, and then I want you to find the open passage through the maze and draw a line along that passageway.'

Pendrake glanced at the figure, saw the open passageway, and drew a line through it. He handed the clipboard back to the psychologist, who glanced at it, startled, but put it down without saying anything.

He now handed Pendrake a sheet with over a thousand little squares on it, arranged in sets of two, one above the other. Each set was numbered, and there were five hundred and ninety-four sets. Dr. Coro said, 'I'm going to read a statement to you for each one of those numbers. If the statement applies to you—that is, if it is correct for you—place an X in the top square. If it's false, place an X in the bottom square. The statement for number one is, "I should like to be a librarian." Is that true or false?'

'False,' said Pendrake.

'Number two,' said the psychologist, 'is, "I like mechanics magazines." True or false?'

Pendrake silently wrote an X in the 'false' square. He looked up and saw that Dr. Coro was watching him. The man said patiently, 'Let's make sure that we understand this test. Will you tell me why you don't wish to be a librarian?'

'They gave me some books here,' said Pendrake, 'and the words distorted every truth that I see in the world and the people around me. So why would I have anything to do with books? Besides, that's a woman's occupation.'

The psychologist parted his lips as if to make a comment, then seemed to think better of it. After a moment's thought he said, 'But that can't apply to mechanics magazines. They describe mechanical processes, and yet you marked that false also. Why?'

'I have a set of mechanics books on that shelf over there,' said Pendrake, indicating the books with his left arm. 'They're too elementary. They tell you how to do things that are obvious.'

'I see,' said Dr. Coro. But he sounded nonplused. He hesitated; then, 'Suppose I were to give you the job of constructing something. How would you go about it?'

'Constructing what?' asked Pendrake, interested.

Dr. Coro reached into his brief case and drew out a rectangular box. He stepped over to the bed and emptied the contents onto the blanket. There were many green plastic shapes in various sizes.

The psychologist said, 'Twenty-seven pieces there, and there's one way of putting them together into a cube. How about trying it?'

Pendrake separated the pieces on the bed, the better to see them. Without pausing, he arranged them in an interlocked pattern that built up in about thirty seconds to a perfect cube. He handed the finished object to Dr. Coro.

The psychologist said in a strained voice, 'How did you do that?'

Pendrake hesitated; he had already forgotten, and he was slightly apologetic. 'Break it down and let me do it again. This time I'll observe the method.'

Dr. Coro silently tumbled the pieces onto the bed. Pendrake handed him the cube twenty seconds later and said, 'It's so much less complex than the way atoms and electrons are fitted together that it isn't a problem. These pieces are shaped to fit one into the other, and so you simply notice which fits which. In putting them together, you're limited only by the speed of your hands.'

The psychologist swallowed hard but asked finally, 'What do you mean, the way atoms and electrons fit together?'

'There's a latticework made of billions of glowing balls,' Pendrake began. He stopped, frowning. 'That's not a good explanation, because it doesn't really tell you what's going on. Consider that desk, for example—the one you're sitting at. When I pervade the area where the legs meet the floor, I see an interesting phenomenon.'

'Pervade?' gasped Dr. Coro.

And that was the way the test went. Some hours later, when Dr. Trevor came in, he was greeted by a very pale young psychologist who said, 'I'm afraid the tests I brought with me are not too suitable for what we have here. According to my tests, he has an IQ of about 500; he is either completely sane or completely insane, and he has an understanding of spatial relationships which seem to operate on an ESP level. I'll have to think about this and come back again in a few days.'

The medico said that all tests should be made while the regenerative growth was in progress, since the entire cell structure seemed to be in a state of special excitement. He predicted that when the growth was completed, 'which should be in a few days now,' there would be a return to normalcy. 'And then,' he went on, 'we will probably find him to be another average person who has to be laboriously taught everything he hasn't carried over from his final minutes as a toti-potent being.'

The doctor took a letter from his pocket. He handed it to his colleague, who read it and handed it back.

'So his name is Pendrake,' said Dr. Coro.

The other man nodded. 'I'll write his wife as soon as the growth is completed. After all, the best thing for him after he's well again will be to be in the hands of someone who knows his background.'

From the bed Pendrake said, 'What did you say my real name is?'

The two men turned and stared at him in surprise. They had acted as if they were in the presence of an object, or at least of something that could not think. And now, like a precocious child, it demanded attention.

Dr. Trevor hesitated and then said, 'James Pendrake. Does the name sound familiar?'

It didn't.

'Say it over and over,' said the doctor, 'until you get used to it.'

'This is your wife,' Mrs. Eleanor Pendrake,' said the doctor with satisfaction.

There had been advance warning of her coming, and so Pendrake gazed with genuine curiosity at the slim, good-looking young woman who stood just inside the door.

He couldn't recall ever having seen her before, but she came quickly, put her arms around him, and kissed his lips. She stepped back. 'It's he,' she said, and she sounded like someone who has emerged from prison gates and is suddenly free. She gazed at the doctor gratefully.

'Thank you for bringing us together,' she said. 'How soon can we get him out of here?'

'Today,' was the reply. 'Since he'll have adequate medical care, the best possible place for him to recover'—he hesitated—'to rebuild his memory, is in his own home. And don't worry—there'll be no publicity. I'll talk to your doctor. As you probably know, the medical association discourages premature publication of case data. We'll make a study of your husband's recovery, but we won't issue a statement for three, four, or perhaps five years from now.'

At no time, then, did Pendrake return to 'normal.' Something of his ability remained. But it was no longer entirely a self-protective condition. Where formerly he had needed only to look at people and things and had no interest in any verbalisms about them, now he craved data as such. Books with their information became important.

In the house on the Pendrake estate in Crescentville his brain was soon subtly misdirected. Eleanor did a womanly thing in that she couldn't refrain from altering the facts of their long separation. Since that required a change in many other personal facts, she soon had a fantasy of tremendous love erected around their past.

She did tell him about his finding of the engine and of their visit to the aerogel towers and of how she had spent some time in a farming colony on Venus. 'They call themselves idealists,' she said indignantly. 'They say they don't want the madness of Earth to be carried to the planets. But they kept me there without my husband. I was the only single woman.'

'But where was I?' Pendrake asked, astonished.

They were preparing for bed late one evening when this conversation took place. Eleanor said nothing until she had slipped into her night clothes, and then she came over to him and said in a troubled voice, 'Some terrible emergency had arisen, and because your body had been exposed to the energies of their space drive, and because you blood type is a rare kind, they had to use you in this emergency. I never understood it, but since this is what made it possible for your arm to grow back, I'm not against them, really. I can't imagine how you escaped them, yet there you were in that hospital.'

Afterward Pendrake lay listening to her gentle breathing and considering the information he now had about himself. It was very little, and he felt completely exposed and vulnerable. For these people who had secretly tried to colonize the planets undoubtedly knew that his permanent home was in Crescentville. Proof: They had transported Eleanor to Earth and then returned her to her home.

They knew—but he didn't.

Before he finally turned over and went to sleep, his mind was made up. The situation could not be left in this blank state.

He had to find out the truth.

Twelve

Pendrake passed under the archway of the drugstore, emerged onto Fiftieth Street—and stopped short.

The twin aerogel towers were across the street, exactly where Eleanor had said they were. He even had a strong sense of familiarity, as if a memory were actually stirring in him. But he dismissed that as fantasy. He accepted that what he knew about himself was exactly what he had been told, and no more.

Nonetheless, after a moment he realized that something was wrong. He saw what it was. Eleanor had said, 'There's a big sign that reads: "Cyrus Lambton Land Settlement Project." '

The sign was not there.

Frowning, Pendrake crossed the street and peered through the window. But the smaller sign that had once graced its interior, giving accurate yet carefully worded details to prospective emigrants—that sign was gone also.

Beyond the window frame, considerably beyond, a woman sat at a desk. Her back was to him, and he assumed without thinking about it that she was Mona Grayson, the daughter of the inventor of the engine.

Pendrake pushed through the door. He had come here today for a chat with Dr. Grayson, and he might as well have it.

'Bin dere anyt'ing you vant?'

The broad German accent was like a slap in the face. Pendrake halted, then slowly walked around to the front of the desk. He stood there staring at the woman.

She had a plump face, dark hair, dark eyes; and after a moment the very grossness of her appearance, the very unvarnished quality of her guttural broken English brought easement to his strained nerves.

He forced himself to reject his critical feelings. After all, there had been plenty of refugee scientists and their families. For all he knew, this was a member of such a family. He said, 'Is Dr. Grayson in?'

'Vot name shall I gif?'

Pendrake winced. 'Pendrake,' he said grudgingly. 'Jim Pendrake.'

'Vrom vere?'

Pendrake made an impatient gesture toward the closed door that led to the other tower. 'Is he in there?'

'I vil send your name if you vill tell me first vere you are vrom. Mr. Birdman vill explain everyt'ing to you.'

'Mr. who?'

'Vun moment, unt I vill call him.'

Pendrake tensed. There was something wrong; just what, wasn't clear. And this comic-opera caricature of an information girl wasn't helping matters. For some reason Grayson and the others had given up these towers as a center of interplanetary activity, and a group of Germans had taken over the building. He looked up with abrupt decision. 'Don't bother to call anyone. I can see I've made a mistake. I——'

He paused, closed his eyes, then opened them again. The pearl-handled revolver was still peering at him over the edge of the woman's desk.

'If you make vun moof,' she said, 'I vill shoot you mit dis noiseless gun.'

A stocky man came into view. He had sandy hair and freckles. His gaze played swiftly over Pendrake, then he said softly in perfect, colloquial American, 'Good work, Lena. I was just beginning to think we'd gathered up all the threads, and now here comes another. We'll put him in a spacesuit, ship him by truck to Field A. There's a plane due there in half an hour. We can quiz him later on. He must have a wife, and maybe some friends.'

After an hour the horrible, jarring ride was over; the chains were taken off the suit that enclosed Pendrake. As he stood up dizzily, he saw a house and other buildings, and standing among them a small cabin-model plane with a jet look to it.

One of the truckmen motioned with a gun. 'Get over there.'

Three men were in the plane. They wore the same kind of metal-plastic suit as Pendrake had on, and they said nothing as he was pushed aboard.

One of them indicated a seat; the man at the controls pushed a lever, and soundlessly the machine began to move forward—and up. The utter silence of the immensely potent movement was all Pendrake needed. Eleanor had described that phenomenon. Here was a Grayson engine.

With startling suddenness the sky grew dark blue. The sun lost its roundness and became a shape of flaring fire in a universe of night.

Behind the plane the Earth began to show its spherical shape. Ahead, the growing orb of the moon glittered.

The phone lights misted with the familiar signal. Birdman picked up the receiver, feeling the empty sensation that always came to him on *this* call.

'Birdman speaking, Excellency.'

The cold voice at the other end said, 'You will be glad to know that after only three days we have all the necessary data on the man Pendrake. As you know, it is imperative that we locate for questioning every person who might have some knowledge of the Grayson engine, and that we do so without creating the slightest suspicion against ourselves. You will therefore see to it that Mrs. Pendrake is kidnaped and taken to the moon. Force her to write some note for her servants, such as that she is joining her husband and may be away for some time.'

'You don't wish her killed?'

'It's unnecessary, on the moon. There's a shortage of women there, as you know. Tell her that she has a month to select a husband from among the permanent workers there.'

The misty light went out. The stocky Birdman shook himself like an animal coming out of a drenching rain. He walked swiftly to a cabinet in one corner of his office. It opened at his touch. Liquor bottles gleamed at him. almost without looking, he snatched one, poured himself a glass of amber stuff, and drained it at a gulp.

He shuddered as the liquid billowed inside him, and then slowly he returned to his desk. Funny, he thought, how the sound of that voice always affected him so strongly.

But he made the arrangements, as directed.

Thirteen

He was lying in darkness.

Pendrake frowned. He remembered the fight with the three Germans—silly fools, they hadn't considered him dangerous!—and he remembered the crash landing on the moon.

He hadn't planned the crash. But things had happened swiftly, and in the final issue there wasn't time to learn exactly how the German controls of the space drive worked.

Yes—the crash, and what had preceded it, was clear enough. It was the darkness that puzzled him.

It was pitch-black; and space hadn't been like that. Space had been a velvet curtain pierced with tiny brilliants; and the sun flashing and flaring through the portholes of the hurtling plane—darkness, but not like this.

Pendrake frowned in bewilderment and tried to move his arm.

It moved reluctantly, as if quicksand were clinging to it. Or as if it were buried in sand——

His mind leaped in an immense comprehension. Powdered pumice stone! He was lying in a 'sea' of settled stone dust somewhere on the side of the moon that eternally faced away from Earth; and all he had to do——

He burst up out of the prison of dust and stood blinking in the ghastly glare of the sun. His heart sank. He was in a vast desert. A hundred yards to his left a plane wing protruded from the sand. To his right, about a third of a mile distant, was a long low ridge across which the sun's rays fell slantwise, creating dense shadows.

The rest was desert. As far as his eyes could see, that dead level of pulverized pumice spread. Pendrake's gaze returned to the exposed wing, and with a stark intensity he thought, 'The engine!' He began to run. His strides were long and bouncy, but he soon learned to balance himself. And hope had come, for damage to the structure of this supership didn't matter. Wings could be torn off, the metal body torn and smashed. But so long as the engine and the drive shaft were intact and attached, the plane would fly.

It was the almost vertical tilt of that wing that fooled him. He used a loose metal plate and excavated doggedly for what must have been half an hour. And then he came to the torn end of the wing.

There was nothing below; no plane, no engine, no tail gear—nothing but pulverized pumice.

The wing poked up into the sky, a mute remnant of a plane that had somehow shed a part of itself and then soared off into eternity. If the laws of chance meant anything, the plane and its engine would fly on forever through space.

But there was still one hope. Pendrake began to walk hurriedly toward the ridge. The slopes of the ridge were steeper than he had estimated, and they were buried in black shadows. Hard to see; he kept sliding back, the loose-packed dust coming down in little rushes. After minutes of effort, he was still only halfway to the top of the two-hundred-foot hill. And it was getting cold. At first the chill hardly touched him, but it swiftly became a biting cold that pressed against his skin and began to steal inside clammily. Within minutes his whole body was numbed, his teeth chattering. He thought in stark amazement: The suit, the damnable suit must be so constructed as to distribute evenly the direct and terrible heat of undiffused sunlight, with no allowance at all for cold.

He reached the top of the ridge and stood with closed eyes facing into the full blaze of the low-hung sun; sluggishly the warmth began to flow back into his veins; he remembered his hope and looked around, looking long and with a gathering desperation. But the plane hadn't merely dropped its wing and then crashed at some near point. In all his scope of vision, the flat reach of pumice sea was unbroken except for seven craters that reared bleakly in the far distance, like witches' mouths sucking at the sky.

He had walked for over an hour toward them, the metal-plate 'shovel' still clutched in his fingers, before it came to Pendrake suddenly that the sun was lower in the sky than it had been.

Night was falling.

He was one man alone running from crater to crater

while a fantastically flaring sun sank lower and lower in a sky that was darker than the midnight heavens of Earth. The extinct volcanoes were all small, the largest only about three hundred yards across. The long shadows from the slanting rays of the sun fell across those crater bottoms; it was only by light reflections from the walls that Pendrake was able to see that here, too, the pumice ocean had spread its silent, enveloping waves of dust.

Two—four, five craters; and still there was no sign of what he was looking for. As with the others, he climbed the sixth from the sunny side and then stood sickly peering down into the black shadows of the shallow pit that spread before him. Pumice, ragged edges of lava, protruding piles of rock that were darker than the shadows that engulfed them—it was all such a familiar pattern now that his eyes made automatic assessment and flashed on in dull dismay.

His gaze was a hundred feet past the cave entrance on the far bottom before he realized that he had succeeded in his search.

He felt himself on the verge of eternity. The rim of the crater seemed sandwiched between the light-sprinkled blackness of space and the hard protrusions of the dead volcano. He raced on. The sun was a blob of flame in a velvet sky. It seemed to quiver to his near right, as if balancing for the downward plunge. Its light cast shadows that seemed longer and more intense with each passing moment; every rill, every unevenness had its own bed of darkness.

Pendrake avoided the shadows. They were wells of cold that numbed his legs when he bounded into them. In his suit was a flashlight, the only thing his captors had provided him with. He turned it on. The sun was a quarter wheel with streamers, an arc-like shape of light standing upright on the ground to his left. The protruding craters were in darkness, a pitlike, mind-shaking darkness. Pendrake shuddered and leaped down to the first level of the cavern. The beam of light from his headpiece showed the floor of pumice dust.

The frightful cold pressed in on him as he dug. Even violent movement wasn't enough now, as it had been so long as part of the sun shone at him. The cold ate at his strength. The plate kept slipping from his numbing hand.

Like a tired old man, he finally lay down in the shallow

trench he had scraped in the dust. With a frantic will he began laboriously to cover himself. His last physical effort came when he pushed his arm through the covering dust and switched off the flashlight. He lay then, his body like a cake of ice, his cheeks curving plates of cold.

The conviction came that he was in his grave.

But the life force in him was tenacious and unyielding. He grew warmer. The ice went out of his bones, his flesh began to tingle, his numbed hand grew fiery with pain, and his fingers thawed. The animal heat of him spread through the suit, a rich, comforting sensation. He couldn't get as warm as he would have liked. The temperature was too low for that. After a long time it struck him that being buried was no solution to anything. He must get deeper, much deeper into the moon's pitted interior.

Lying there in his lonely pumice grave, Pendrake became aware of a strange feeling, the feeling that he knew something, that all was not lost, that there was a way for him to go. His reasoning mind fastened on this eerie feeling and from it constructed a belief that he must actually be very near the secret East German base on the moon.

The Germans, too, must have gone into the interior. It would be warmer farther down. Friction alone, the friction of semiviscid rock and metal, product of the moon's own tortuous writhings, would create a special higher temperature which would be held in by the insulating pumice and lava of the surface. There was, of course, the problem of how to get food and water, but with a perfect spaceship engine they could transport what they needed.

Pendrake was struggling now to get out of his burial plot, and so he pushed other thoughts out of his mind. Climbing to his feet, he switched on his light and began to work his way down.

The path was a twisted one, as if once the cave might have been the tubular funnel of a live volcano—pulled out of shape by the shifting of the moon's crust. Down, down, slantingly down. Of how many times he sought warmth in a bed of dust, Pendrake has no memory. Twice he slept; for how long, he had no idea at all. It could have been a minute's doze: it might have been hours each time.

The cave was timeless. A world of night through which

the light from his helmet poked at intervals like a thin flame. He had no mercy on himself, but plunged down, often at a dead run, after a brief flicking on of his light to reveal possible dangers. Other caves began to branch off from the main cavern. Sometimes they were plainly nothing but branches. But when a possibility of confusion existed, Pendrake forced himself to stop, to stand there while the hideous cold ate into him—stand there and clearly mark an arrow to indicate the direction from which he had come.

He slept again, and then again. Five days, he thought, and knew that he might be fooling himself. A body so subjected to deathly cold must need more sleep than normal to recuperate. All his great strength could not ward off such a reaction of the human system. But five sleeps—five days. Grimly he counted them in full and added each sleep as one day—six, seven, eight, nine——

Gradually it grew warmer. For a long, long time he didn't notice that. But finally the consciousness penetrated that the intervals between those frantic burials were lengthening. It was still bitterly cold on the tenth 'day,' but the chill was a slower pressure, not a biting, numbing thing. The warmth stayed longer inside him. For the first time he could walk along and clearly realize that he was mad to continue into this eternal night.

Other thoughts came, too. He ought to give up the hope that safety was still farther ahead of him. He ought to start back toward the surface, where he could make a desperate search for one of the German camps. That was the logical thing to do, so he reasoned.

But the thoughts did not trigger the action, for he kept on moving forward.

There were moments in the hours that followed when Pendrake forgot what his hope was, and there were bitter hours when he cursed the intensity of the life force that drove him in this desperate search. But the very vagueness of his plans eroded his will, already long weakened from the pangs of hunger and by a thirst so terrible that every minute seemed an hour; every second, hell.

Turn around, his mind said. But his feet went on unheeding, down and down. He stumbled. He fell. And got up again. He made the narrow hairpin turn that led to the lighted corridor, almost unseeing. And he was actually stepping across the entrance before the reality of it penetrated.

Pendrake dived behind a big up-jut of rock. He lay there quivering, so weak, so ill from reaction, that for minutes his only thought was:

The end had come.

Recovery came hard. His nervous energy, that extraordinary reservoir of his great strength, was exhausted. But after a while his spirit surged once more into life. Cautiously he peered over the needle of rock behind which his spacesuit-clad body clumped. He was crazy, of course, to think that he had seen moving shapes in the distance, but——

The corridor stretched before his gaze on a gradual downward slant. His first intense glance showed that it was empty of life. It took a long moment after that to grasp that it wasn't lighted by electric bulbs and that his initial impression, that light meant Germans, was wrong.

He was alone in an old cave deep inside Earth's satellite, like a worm that had crawled along a dried-out artery of somebody's crumbling flesh.

The radiance from the walls was not even in texture, nor was it spaced according to any distinguishable pattern. As he walked cautiously forward, points and splashes of light shone at him. There was a long, trembly line on the right wall and a rough crescent on the left, and other shapeless and meaningless forms glowed and blinked along the corridor as far as the eye could see. Pendrake thought sharply: Some kind of radiant ore which might be harmful——

Harmful! His bitter laughter echoed inside his headpiece, cut new cracks into his thirst-swollen lips, and ended abruptly as the pain grew unbearable. A man on the verge of death didn't have to worry about new dangers. He plunged on, for a while heedless. And then slowly the presence of light penetrated anew. The truth burst upon him suddenly as he paused at a turning and found himself staring down a long slant at a corridor of light that faded into a point of distance.

The corridor was artificial!

And old! Fantastically old. So old that the walls, which

must have been as smooth as glass and harder than anything human beings had ever made, walls radiant in every element, had crumbled before the eroding pressure of countless centuries. Crumbled; and this sheltered, twisted, light-splotched tunnel was the result.

He stumbled on, and the cunning thought came that the radiance would enable him to save his flashlight. For some obscure reason, that seemed immensely important. He began to giggle. It seemed suddenly irresistibly comic that he who was about to die had happened at this ultimate moment of his life upon an underground universe where beings had once lived.

His giggling became a wild, uncontrollable glee. Finally, however, it ended from sheer exhaustion, and he leaned weakly against the wall, staring down at the tiny river that washed across the cave, burbling out of a big crack in the rock and whirling out of sight into a hole in the opposite wall. 'I'll just cross that stream,' he told himself confidently, 'and then——'

Stream! The shock of awareness was so terrible in the nausea it brought that he staggered and fell like a stunned animal. The crash of metal and plastic on rock resounded in his ears; and the impact, the clangor brought back a measure of his sanity.

He grew more alert, more conscious, came farther out of his stupor.

Water! The surprise of its presence struck him more sharply. The thought, the comprehension grew so big that it projected clear through his brain and down into his muscles and was still too big. Water! *And running!* Come to think of it, there hadn't been any cold for a long time. Have to get his head free, air or no air. Somehow he'd survive if he got the water.

He climbed unsteadily to his feet and saw the men coming toward him. He blinked at them, thought finally in a frowning astonishment: 'No armor, no headpieces! Queerly dressed, though. Funny!'

Before he could think further, there was a scramble of footsteps behind him. He whirled to see a dozen men bearing down from that direction. Instantly, knives flashed. A raucous voice yelled:

'Kill the dern critter. Dirty furrin' spy!'

'Hey!' Pendrake breathed hoarsely.

His voice was lost in a chorus of bloodthirsty yells. He was shoved, flung; and he hadn't the strength even to lift his arm. At the very moment that the club struck him a slanting head blow, his amazement reached its peak; amazement because——

His assailants were not German!

Fourteen.

Four years had gone by since Pendrake found the engine that afternoon of August 1972; nearly a year had now passed from the time that he escaped from Jefferson Dayles's amazons, most of it spent with Eleanor, recuperating and regrowing his arm once more. Again, it was summer. In this month of August 1976, to all outward appearances not a clue existed as to the fate of a missing airman and his kidnaped wife. In all those vital days, no one seemed interested in the whereabouts of Mr. and Mrs. James Pendrake.

But there was a clue.

August 1976 ended. The Earth sighed with ten thousand winds. September 1 flashed across the international date line. By the time it reached the eastern American seaboard a north-easter was blowing, and a score of meteorologists drew their isobars and noted laconically that winter would be early this year.

By midafternoon of September 1 the hidden clue was discovered. Air Commissioner Blakeley recovered from a bad case of influenza and returned to his office. In catching up on events, he came across a file on a Mrs. Pendrake. The name did not at once stir any memory. 'Why is this on my desk?' he asked his secretary.

'That woman tried to contact you while you were ill,' was the reply. 'She was quite hysterical and babbled something about an atomic engine and an organization that was transporting emigrants to Venus. It all sounded mad, but when I tried to get in touch with her yesterday at her home I was informed that she had left without telling anyone. A note was found later, but the servant who told me this said it didn't really look like Mrs. Pendrake's normal handwriting. In view of your previous contact with the Pendrakes—that is, with Mr. Pendrake—I thought I'd better bring it to your attention.'

Blake nodded and leaned back. 'Pendrake!' he mused. Then flushed with remembered humiliation. 'That was the one-armed man who threw me out of his house, then some time afterward sent me a list of names and addresses of atomic scientists——'

His thought poised there in a dreadful premonition. A storm of blood hammered at his temples. 'This could ruin me!' he thought. After a little while, very white, he went through the Pendrake file and reread the letter with its list of names: Dr. McClintock Grayson, Cyrus Lambton—— Come to think of it, he'd read about the death of those men in an accident.... This thing looked bigger every instant. Sweating, he read his own reply to Pendrake's letter. '... Further correspondence would be useless——'

For a long minute he stared down at the damning document. Finally his jaw stiffened. He reached for his buzzer, pressed it firmly, and said, 'First get me Cree Lipton of the Federal Bureau of Investigation, and then call Ned Hoskins, the patent attorney——'

The stocky man reached the hotel through the secret entrance. He felt himself scrutinized, but finally the door swung open. He was led along a corridor. A few minutes later he was in the inner sanctum.

'Excellency!' he bowed.

The tall, gaunt man who sat behind a large metal desk in an office overlooking Fifth Avenue stared at him from eyes that were like shining holes in his head, they were so hard and bright. 'Herr Birdman,' he said, 'the FBI are investigating the disappearance of Mrs. Pendrake. They have already found that a plane landed and took off straight up. That should have been forbidden.'

The stocky man gurgled his dismay. 'Perhaps the men had no choice. Sometimes quick departures are necessary.'

'I am not interested in reasons.' The cold voice was implacable. 'Only one thing saves these men from severe punishment. As yet, no one connects us with the matter, and so perhaps as a final precaution the time has come to burn certain buildings under Plan D2. We must make sure nothing remains to incriminate us. See to it.'

'It shall be done, Excellency, at once.'

'One more point. About Pendrake himself—we must not assume that he is dead. His trail from the shattered plane wing led to a cave in the crater. A cursory investigation showed that he was still alive at a depth of one mile but that he was burying himself at intervals, and so we may assume that the automatic heating mechanism of his spacesuit was damaged in the crash.

'To make sure of him, I think we must now be prepared to organize a military campaign against the cave dwellers. We have tolerated their depredations long enough....'

Pendrake awakened to the sound of a melodious humming. It was somewhere off to his left, but for the moment the delicious weakness of his every nerve and muscle, the old physical pleasure of lying on something soft and comfortable, diminished the inclination in him to turn his head and look at the man whose tuneful warbling had aroused him.

After a moment it struck Pendrake with a sharp consciousness that he was alive, and that didn't fit in with what had gone before.

But still he lay there. And after a little he found himself frowning in amazement at a lighted cave roof that must have been a mile high. He closed his eyes, shook himself as if to clear his brain of any fantasy, then opened his eyes again. The tremendous roof was still there. What had been a narrow snake of a cave had somehow opened out, and here was an underground vastness.

The sight quickened his whole being. He grew aware of a thin breeze that touched him and brought a sweet scent of growing things, an odor of garden and trees in bloom. Pendrake stirred in a gathering excitement. The movement brought his first awareness that he was no longer arrayed in the spacesuit.

The movement did something else. It ended the humming. Footsteps sounded. A young man's voice said, 'Oh, you're awake.'

The speaker came into view. He was a slight-built young man with a thin face and bright eyes. He wore a curiously old-fashioned, threadbare coat, and his legs were encased in trousers that were strapped under his shoes. He said, 'You've been unconscious for four sleep periods. I've been squeezing water and fruit juices between your lips every little while. My name's Morrison, by the way.'

'I was lost,' said Pendrake, and blinked as he said it, for no words had come, only a hoarse, rasping sound.

'Better not try to speak yet,' the young man counseled. 'You're still pretty poorly. As soon as you're strong enough you're to be taken to Big Oaf for questioning—that's why you've been kept alive.'

The words didn't penetrate right away. Pendrake lay very still, thinking: The cold and his will to live had kept him going. And so he was alive. As for this fellow, Big Oaf——

Big *what*?

He muttered his amazement and this time managed a husky whisper. The young man grinned at him. 'That's his name, all right. Somebody called him that once, and he took a fancy to it, and nobody's ever dared to tell him the meaning. He's Neanderthal, you know. Been here a million years, at least, almost as long as the devil-beast in the pit.'

A startled look came over the young man's face. 'Oh!' he said in alarm. 'I wasn't supposed to tell you that.' He was suddenly in a panic. Gasping, he came down beside Pendrake, clawed at his arm. 'For heaven's sake,' he whispered hoarsely, 'don't tell anybody that I told you how old we are down here. I've done my best for you. I've brought you back to life; I fed you. I was supposed to keep you locked up—I'm your guard, you know, and you're in jail. But I brought you out here and——' He broke off. 'Please don't tell!'

His face was a twisted mask of fear—which changed. Changed to cunning, then to ferocity. Abruptly he jerked at the knife that Pendrake saw for the first time was in a sheath under his coat. 'If you don't promise,' he threatened wildly, 'I'll have to pretend that you tried to escape and that I had to kill you.'

Pendrake found his voice. 'Of course I promise,' he whispered. He saw instantly in the distorted eyes above him that no simple promise could soothe the terrified creature who crouched over him. Danger made his whisper louder, stronger, as he said swiftly, 'Don't you see, if I know something they don't want me to know, it's to my own interest to keep the information to myself. You see that, don't you?'

Slowly the fear died out of the young man's eyes. He climbed shakily to his feet then he began to whistle softly. Finally he said, 'They're going to toss you to the devil-beast anyway. They take no chances except with the women. But keep my name out of it, that's all, and anything I've said.'

'Agreed!'

Pendrake whispered the word and mustered the form of a

smile, but he was thinking grimly: 'Sleep lightly. Watch out for a knife—in my sleep.'

He must have slept even as that thought was still forming in his mind.

His first consideration when he awakened the second time was: A man named Morrison—in the center of the moon. These men came from Earth and had been here a long time. It was a strange phenomenon, and he must quickly find out more about it.

There was a sound beside him. A thin, familiar face bent over him. 'Uh!' said Morrison. 'You're awake again. I've been waiting, listening to you talking in your sleep, and you talked a lot. I'm supposed to report everything you say.'

Pendrake started to nod half to himself, his mind merely taking in the words; and then the larger meaning of them, the mental picture of someone—out there—someone named Big Oaf giving orders, cunningly receiving the reports of spies, granting temporary stays of execution—— Abruptly he felt outraged. He sat up. 'Look here,' he began, 'who the devil——' His voice was clear and strong, but it wasn't the awareness of returned strength that stopped him short. What happened was that as he raised himself he saw a scene that had not been visible when he was lying down.

Below him was a town set in a garden of trees and flowers. There were broad streets, and he could see men and —queer—uniformed women.

He forgot the people of the town. His gaze soared from horizon to horizon. There was a green meadow on the far side of the town where cattle grazed. Beyond, the ceiling of the cave swept down to a junction with the ground at some point below the cliff, a point invisible from where he sat.

It held him for a moment, that line where radiant cave sky met a cave horizon.

Then his gaze came back to the pretty town. It began a hundred feet away. First there was a line of tall trees heavily laden with large gray fruit. The trees sheltered the nearest of many buildings. The structure was small, delicate-looking. It seemed to have been built of some shell-like substance. It glowed as if light were inside it, shining through its translucent walls. Its design was more that of a shapely bee's nest than of a sea shell, but the resemblance to the

shell was there, too. The other buildings that glinted tanta-
lizingly through the trees differed widely in details, but the
central architectural motif, and the basic glow-material,
were ever present.

'The town's been like that,' Morrison's voice said, 'since I
came in 1853, and Big Oaf says it was like that when
he——'

Pendrake turned. The mention of dates was staggering,
but he caught at the wedge they offered. 'And he's been
around a million years, you said.'

The thin face twisted uneasily. The man looked hastily
around. His hand crept toward his knife. Then he caught
Pendrake's eye, and he let go of the hilt. He was trembling,
'Don't repeat that,' he whispered desperately. 'I was mad to
tell you, but it just came out, that's all. It just came out.'

There was no mistaking the fear. It was real, and it made
everything else real—the million years, Big Oaf, the eternal
town below. For a long second Pendrake stared at the way
the weakling's face was working, then he said, 'I won't say a
word, but I do want to know what it's all about. How did
you get here onto the moon?'

Morrison shifted. A bead of sweat ran down his cheeks;
Pendrake felt a stark incredulity that any man could be so
frightened. 'I can't tell you,' Morrison said in a panicky
voice. 'They'll throw me to the beast, too. Big Oaf's been
saying that there's too many of us here ever since we ab-
ducted those German girls.'

'German girls!' Pendrake ejaculated, and stopped himself
short, his eyes narrowed to pin points. That accounted for the
women in uniform he had seen in the streets. But what a
hornet's nest these cave dwellers were stirring up for themselves!

Morrison was continuing, his tone sharp: 'Big Oaf and his
cronies are mad for women. Big Oaf's got five wives now,
not counting the two that killed themselves, and he sent
another kidnaping expedition out. When they get back—
well, he's just waiting for a chance to kill off all the decent
men.'

The picture was clearer now; the missing details fundamentally unimportant. Pendrake sat grim and cold, mentally
visualizing the cataclysm that had brought hell to the

moon's Garden of Eden. These fools, Morrison and the others like him, he thought, were waiting like a herd of frightened sheep for the slaughter, even humming happy little tunes to pass the time. He parted his lips to speak—and was cut off by a bull voice, behind him, roaring, 'What's this, Morrison? The prisoner strong enough to sit up and you haven't reported it! Get going, stranger. I'm taking you to Big Oaf.'

For a moment Pendrake sat as still as death. The needle-sharp thought that came finally was: 'He was too sick, too weak. The crisis had come too soon.

Nevertheless, he was alert as he walked along the street of the village. That he could walk at all was relieving. He dared not try anything involving strength yet, but he must survive a few 'days' longer—gain time to observe, correlate, and organize the frightened 'decent' men who, according to Morrison, were destined for slaughter. He wasted scarcely a glance at the houses, and the motley assortment of raggedly dressed men and the sullen women in their German women's corps uniforms barely touched the outer fringes of his thought. His mind, his whole being was concentrated on trying to locate key bastions of the town.

With abrupt understanding of the military-like regulations of vital supplies that were here, he noted that two half-naked men with blue skins and broad flat noses stood guard over a stream of water that gushed from a wall and gurgled out of sight through a hole in the ground. There were other places being guarded, particularly four large buildings, but the reasons for protecting them were not apparent at first glance.

Pendrake moved forward a few yards, then stopped. And stared. In almost the exact center of the town, half hidden by a growth of trees, was a stockade. It was made of tree boles lashed together. Tall it stood, presenting a hundred-and-fifty-foot front, fifty feet high, with a massive gate around which loitered a dozen men with spears, longbows, and drawn knives. The structure looked incongruous among the delicate-hued, shell-like houses. But there was no doubt at all that here in this monstrous fort dwelt the central authority of this world within a world.

The thought ended as one of the guards, a raggedly

dressed individual who wore spurs on high boots and looked like a bad caricature of a cowboy, challenged, 'Takin' this feller to see Big Oaf, Troger?'

'Yep!' Pendrake's bearded, bull-voiced escort answered. 'You better search him, though.'

'What about Morrison? Does he go in too?' asked a dark-eyed man in a shiny tattered remnant of what must once have been a black suit of some kind. It struck Pendrake with a start, as fingers poked eagerly through his pockets, that this second guard resembled with startling fidelity a motion-picture version he had seen of a gambler of the Old West.

Pendrake felt a sudden, sharp fascination. In spite of himself, in spite of his will to bestow not one glance on anything that might confuse, he grew aware of the men. They had been a blur of his vision; now they came into sharp focus: men of all periods of the West, an astounding assortment, even some who didn't seem to fit at all.

But Pendrake felt not a shadow of doubt. They were all western American. It was as if a net had been cast from the moon, and into that net had fallen men from the middle period of development of the western United States; and then the catch had been gathered here and, like this immortal village, kept immune from the ravages of time. There were about a hundred men visible from where he stood at the gate of the stockade. Seven of them were Indians in loincloths, red of skin, tall, arrow-backed. They *fitted*. And so did all the roughly dressed men in open-necked shirts and belted, narrow-legged trousers, and so did the ragged cowboys.

Morrison didn't fit, not quite, though there undoubtedly had been clerkish types like him in western towns. There were some short, ugly men and some very fine big, dark brown men who didn't fit either; and there was another one of the half-naked, blue-skinned, flat-nosed men. One thing seemed clear. Whoever had collected this crew had gotten hold of some of the toughest characters that the old, hard West had ever bred.

A big hand grabbed his collar, pushed him physically and mentally out of his mood of appraisal. 'Get in there!' said the voice of Troger.

Pendrake's reaction was automatic. If he had thought, if

he hadn't had to come so far out of his dark speculations, he would have controlled himself in time. But the insult of being grabbed and shoved came too suddenly. His response was as violent as it was involuntary. One arm came up, his fingers caught the offending wrist, and for a brief instant every tired nerve in his body pumped power into his muscles.

There was a roar of pain and a hard thud as Troger described a cartwheel in the air and landed twenty feet away. The man bounced up instantly, raging, 'I'll beat your brains out! No guy can——'

He stopped; his gaze fastened on somebody behind Pendrake, and his whole body grew rigid. Pendrake, trembling from the nausea produced by his effort and dismayed by his stupidity in revealing how strong he could be, turned dizzily.

A creature stood in the gate, and one glance was enough to identify it: Here was Big Oaf, Neanderthal monstrosity.

He was a man. He had a roughly human shape, a head with eyes, nose, and mouth. But at that point the physical resemblance to anything human ended. His figure was five feet four in height and about three feet wide in the chest. His arms hung below his knees. His face was—beast; the teeth far too long and projecting from between enormously thick lips.

He stood there like some creature out of a primeval jungle, naked and hairy except for a black fur that hung from a strap around his belly. He stood slouching, and it took a long moment for Pendrake to grasp that the creature's piglike eyes were studying him shrewdly. Even as realization came, the thing parted those tremendous lips and said in throaty but unmistakable English, 'Bring the feller inside! I'll talk to him from my throne. Let about fifty people in.'

Inside the stockade was a big, glowing, shell-like house, a little river of gurgling water, fruit trees, a vegetable garden, and a wooden dais on which stood a huge wooden chair.

The wooden chair was the throne, and it was obvious to the grim Pendrake that whoever had given Big Oaf the idea of kingship hadn't had too clear an idea of regal splendor.

But Big Oaf seated himself with assurance and said, 'What's your handle?'

It was no time for resistance. Pendrake gave his name quietly.

Big Oaf whirled in his chair, pointed with a thick hairy finger at a tall gray-eyed man in a faded black suit. 'What kind of a handle is that, MacIntosh?'

The tall man shrugged. 'English.'

'Oh!' The pig eyes turned back to Pendrake, stared speculatively. The beast said, 'Better talk fast, stranger.'

The western twang of speech made it almost impossible for Pendrake to grasp that he was on trial. It was a psychological hurdle that he had to force his mind over. But finally, with gathering consciousness that he was talking for his life, Pendrake began his explanation. He finished with a rush, twisting on his heel and facing straight toward the thin-faced young man who had been his jailer, saying in a ringing voice, 'And Morrison, here, will bear out every word. He says I talked in my delirium about what I'd been through. Isn't that right, Morrison?'

Pendrake stared at the young man's face and felt a brief, icy sardonicism at the petrified expression that was there. Morrison's eyes grew wide and then Morrison was gulping, 'Yup, that's right, Big Oaf. You 'member you told me to listen, and that's what he said. He——'

'Shurrup!' said Big Oaf, and Morrison collapsed into silence like a pricked balloon.

Pendrake felt no regret at all that he had put pressure on the little coward. He saw that the monster was studying him intently, and there was something in the expression— Pendrake forgot Morrison as Big Oaf said in a strangely gentle voice:

'Hit him a little, guys: I like to see how a feller takes punishment.'

After a minute he said, 'All right, that'll do.'

Pendrake climbed groggily to his feet, and it wasn't all acting. In the excitement of the—trial—he had forgotten that he was a sick man. He stood shakily and heard the beast-man say, 'Well, fellers, what'll we do with him?'

'Kill him!' It was a raucous cry from several throats. 'Throw him to the devil-beast. We ain't had a show for a long time.'

'That ain't no reason to kill anybody,' said a lean man in

the back of the crowd. 'If these fellers had their way, they'd have a show every week, and we'd all be dead soon.'

'Yah, Chris Devlin,' a man snarled, 'and that's just what you'll be one of these days.'

'Just start something!' Devlin snapped back. 'We're waitin' for ya.'

'That'll do!' It was Big Oaf. 'The stranger lives. You can stay with Morrison for a while. And lissen, Pendrake, I wanna talk to you after you've had another sleep. Hear that, you guys? Let him in when he comes. Now beat it, all of you.'

Pendrake was outside the stockade almost before he realized that he had been granted life.

Sixteen

Pendrake ate and slept, then ate and slept again.

He awakened from his third sleep with the realization that he must not delay any longer his visit to Big Oaf.

But he lay there for a few minutes. It was not that his bedroom was particularly comfortable. The sparkling light from the walls was too sustained for human eyes that needed darkness when resting. The bed, while soft, was concave. So were the two long, backless chairs. The door that led to the adjoining room was two feet high, like an igloo entrance.

There was a scraping sound. A head poked through the doorway, and a lean, long man crawled inside and stood up. It took a moment for Pendrake to recognize Chris Devlin, the man who had objected to his being killed. Devlin said, 'I'm being watched. So my coming here puts you under suspicion.'

'Good,' said Pendrake.

'Eh!' The man stared at him, and Pendrake returned his gaze coolly. Devlin went on slowly: 'You've been thinking things over, I see!'

'Plenty,' said Pendrake.

Devlin seated himself in one of the concave chairs, 'Say-y-y,' he said, 'you're a man after my own heart. I'd like to ask you a question: The way you handled Troger—was that an accident?'

'I could do that,' said Pendrake flatly, 'to Big Oaf.'

He saw that Devlin was impressed, and he smiled wryly at the effectiveness of the psychology he had used—the psychology of deliberate positivity.

'It's too bad,' said Devlin, 'that a man of your spirit is a little dumb. No one man can take on Big Oaf. Besides, he'll avoid a direct attack.'

Pendrake said quickly, 'The important thing is, how many men can you count on?'

'About a hundred. Two hundred more would shift over if they dared, but they'll wait till the tide has turned. That leaves two hundred solidly against us, and they can probably dragoon another hundred into fighting for them.'

'A hundred's enough,' said Pendrake. 'The world is run by small groups of men. Five hundred determined men and two hundred thousand dupes overthrew the Czarist regime in a Russia of a hundred and fifty million people. Hitler took control of Germany with a comparatively small body of active followers. But here's some advice, Devlin.'

'Yes?'

'Take the water source. Take the places that are guarded, and hold them at all costs. Get the cattle!' Pendrake paused; then, 'How many wives have you got, Devlin?'

The man started, changed color. He said at last, violently, 'We'd better leave the women out of this, Pendrake. Our men have been so long without women that—we'd lose all our followers.'

'How many wives?' said Pendrake steadily.

Devlin stared at him. He was pale now, his voice harsher. 'Big Oaf's been clever,' he admitted. 'When we captured those German women he gave every one of his hundred most determined enemies two wives.'

'Tell your men,' Pendrake said, 'to choose the one they prefer and leave the other alone. Do you understand?'

Devlin was on his feet. 'Pendrake,' he said in a thick voice, 'I'm warning you, leave this subject be. It's dynamite.'

'You fool!' Pendrake snapped at him. 'Don't you see that you've got to start right? The human mind has a tendency to get into certain habits. If the habits are wrong—and the way these women were handed over makes chattel out of them and is therefore utterly wrong—I repeat, if the habits are wrong, you can't just start refashioning the mind. You've got to break *that* matrix by death and begin with a fresh one——' He broke off. 'Besides, you people haven't any choice. You're all slated to be killed, and those wives are designed to keep you quiet until the right opportunity occurs. You know that, don't you?'

Devlin nodded reluctantly. 'I guess you're right.'

'You bet I'm right,' said Pendrake coldly. 'And I might as well make my position clear : Either this game is played my way, or it's played without me'—he stood up with a swift, gliding movement, his voice grim as he finished—'and I pity those who tackle Big Oaf without these muscles of mine to hold him off. Well, what do you say?'

Devlin was standing frowning at the floor. At last he looked up, a wan smile on his face. 'You win, Pendrake. I don't promise results, but I'll do my derndest. Our boys are good fellers at heart—and at least they'll know they're dealing with a right guy. But now you'd better be on your way to Big Oaf. Yell loud if he starts anything.'

'Any idea,' asked Pendrake, 'what he wants me for?'

'Nary a one,' was the reply, and Pendrake was halfway to the stockade before it occurred to him that he still didn't know how these Old West men had gotten to the moon, and that he had forgotten to ask Devlin if the cave dwellers had had the wit to make plans to protect themselves from German retaliation for their depredations.

So quickly had he become absorbed by the immediate danger and forgetful of the greater, more remote one.

He was admitted through the gate of the stockade silently. A few minutes later Big Oaf crawled out of the door of his house and stood up. 'You took your time,' he growled.

'I'm a sick man,' Pendrake explained, 'and this moon gravity makes it possible to walk where you'd be flat on your back on Earth. That beating your men handed me didn't help any, either.'

The monster's answer was a grunt, and Pendrake stared at him cautiously. They were alone inside the stockade, and the effect was of isolation from the universe, a curious, empty feeling of being cut off in an unnatural world.

He saw with a start that the creature's small eyes were studying him. Big Oaf broke the silence. 'I been here a long time, Pendrake, a long time. I was kinda foolish when I first came—like these other guys are—but my brain somehow grew up over the years, and now I got the sense to worry about things they never even think about, like those Germans, f'r instance.'

He paused and looked at Pendrake. Pendrake hesitated, said finally, 'You'd better worry about them and worry hard.'

Big Oaf waved an apelike arm and shrugged his massive shoulders. 'I merely mentioned that as a f'r instance. I got my plans laid for those fellers. What I mean is, when you look at me, think of somebody who's got a brain with sense in it like your own, and never mind the body. How about it, uh?'

Pendrake blinked. The appeal was so unexpected, so remarkable in the picture it brought of a sensitive mind aware of the beastlike body, that he was touched in spite of himself. Then he remembered the five wives and the two other women who had killed themselves. He said slowly, 'What other worries have you got, Big Oaf?'

It seemed to him as he spoke the noncommittal words that the barest hint of disappointment flickered over the hairy face. Then Big Oaf said, 'I was walkin' along a trail on Earth 'n' all of a sudden I was here.'

'What's that!' Pendrake gasped.

Incredulous, his mind darted back over the apeman's words, and again the shock came. It took him a long moment to realize that he had been told the secret of how these people had arrived on the moon.

Big Oaf was continuing, 'It was the same with the others, 'n' from the way they describe it, they were comin' down the same trail. That scares me, Pendrake.'

Pendrake frowned. 'What do you mean?'

'There's somethin' down there on Earth, nothin' you can see, but at this end you come out of a machine. Pendrake, we gotta shut off that machine somehow. We can't live here, not knowin' who or what's gonna barge along that trail and through the machine.'

'I see what you mean,' said Pendrake thoughtfully.

It was the calmness of his own words that shocked him this time. For he was quivering in every nerve, his whole body cold, then hot, then cold again. A machine—a machine that transported objects unharmed—focused on a trail in the western United States, a machine through which an army could come and attack the Communist strongholds on the moon, capture an engine, everything——

With a start Pendrake saw that the Neanderthal was glaring at him. The man had been sitting against the edge of the wooden platform on which the throne chair stood; now he leaned forward; the great muscles of his chest stood out like anchor ropes. 'Stranger,' he said, and he almost hissed the words, 'get this straight, this place is fenced-in territory. There ain't never a lot of people gonna come down here. The world'd go mad if it was ever found out that there's a town in the moon where it's possible to live forever. Now, do you see why we've got to shut off that machine and cut ourselves off from the outside? We got somethin' down here that people'd commit murder to have.

'Wait'—his voice beat at Pendrake—'I'm gonna show you what happens to guys who get any other kind of idea. Come along.'

Pendrake came. Big Oaf ran along the street straight into the open country, and Pendrake, bounding along behind, saw after a moment where he was heading : the cliff.

Big Oaf reached it first. He pointed down. 'Look,' he cried hoarsely.

Pendrake approached the edge of the abyss cautiously and peered over. He found himself staring down a wall of cliff that descended smooth and straight for a distance of several hundred feet. There was brush at the bottom and a grassy plain and——

Pendrake gasped. Then he felt dizzy. He swayed, then with an effort caught his whirling mind. And looked again, trembling.

The yellow-green-blue-red beast in the pit was sitting on its haunches. It looked as big as a horse. Its head was tilted, its baleful eyes glaring up at the two men. And the hideously long teeth that protruded from its jaws confirmed Pendrake's instant identification.

The devil-beast was a saber-toothed tiger.

Slowly Pendrake's breathing returned to normal, his pounding heart slowed. The great wonder came : how many aeons that machine must have been focused on that trail there on Earth to have caught such a prehistoric monster. And how long ago the people who had built the machine and the village must have died.

Another thought came, an immensely strange and disturbing idea, actually more a fear, a feeling, a shrinking of his flesh than a thought-concept. It was an essence of primeval memory in him which uttered a shriek of terror and disbelief, as if each cell cried out in horror : 'For God's sake, I thought we had outlived that nightmare long ago.' The cells remembered an ancient enemy and cringed with instinctual panic.

Pendrake licked his dry lips, and this time he had a conscious realization : 'Of course the danger from the beast world is not over. Man is in a struggle to conquer not only the beasts and the disorder of Nature but his own deep-rooted animal impulses.'

The thought passed. With narrowed eyes he stared at Big Oaf. The creature-man was kneeling at the abyss edge a dozen feet away, watching him intently. Pendrake said softly, 'It must have been fed. It must have been kept alive on purpose.'

Blue-gray eyes that were slate-hard met his own. 'At first,' said Big Oaf, 'I kept it alive for company. I used to sit on the cliff and shout at it. Then when the blue men came with a bunch of buffalo, I got the idea that maybe it would come in handy. It knows me now.' He finished darkly, 'There's plenty of men inside it, and there'll be more. Better not be one of them, Pendrake.'

Pendrake said steadily, slowly, 'I'm beginning to see the light. All this attention you're lavishing on me—you said something about shutting off the machine—and I'm the only man who ever came here who knows anything about machinery. Am I getting warm, Big Oaf?'

Big Oaf climbed to his feet, and Pendrake did the same. They backed away from the cliff's edge step by step, staring at each other. It was Big Oaf who spoke first. 'You ain't the first, but the others ain't around no more.' He paused; then, 'Pendrake, I'm gonna offer you half of everything. Me and you'll be the bosses here, with first choice of the women an' all the good things. You know we can't let the world in on this place. It just ain't possible. We'll live here forever, and maybe if you ever get all the machines on this place workin' we can step out and get what we want from anywhere.'

Pendrake said, 'Big Oaf, have you ever heard of an election?'

'Uh!' The pig eyes stared at him suspiciously. 'What's that?'

Pendrake explained, and the hairy beast gaped at him. 'You mean,' he exploded, 'if those lame-brains don't like the way I run things they could kick me out?'

'That's it,' said Pendrake. 'And it's the only way I'll play ball.'

'To hell with that,' was the snarling response. And on the way back to the town Big Oaf said in an ugly tone: 'Somebody told me you been talkin' to Devlin, Pendrake. You——' He broke off. The anger died from him as if he had cut it out with a surgical knife, cleanly. As Pendrake watched the transformation in narrow-eyed astonishment, a grin spread over the apelike face. 'Just lissen to me gettin' mad,' Big Oaf said, 'a feller that's lived a million years and is gonna live another million if he plays his cards straight.'

Pendrake was silent, conscious of the man eying him. He was startled, too, thoughtful. In every way Big Oaf was showing himself to be an immensely dangerous 'feller.'

'I got all the aces, Pendrake,' Big Oaf's voice projected softly across his brief reverie, 'and a royal flush up my sleeve. I can't get killed 'less a rock falls down from the roof——' He glanced up toward the height above, then looked at Pendrake, his grin broader. 'It happened once to a guy.'

They had stopped. They stood in a little valley under a spread of trees. The town was beyond the rim of the hill. But for the moment there was not a sound of laughter, not a whisper of voices. They were alone in a queer universe, man and semi-man facing each other.

Pendrake broke the thrall. 'I'm not going to count on it happening to you.'

Big Oaf guffawed. 'Now you're smart. I thought you'd catch on quick. Lissen, Pendrake, you can't buck me, so think over what I've told you. Meantime I want your promise you won't mix up with anybody. Is that fair?'

'Absolutely,' said Pendrake. He felt no compunction about the swift promise. It was clear that he had gone to the very edge of the abyss in his opposition, and he wasn't ready. If there was one thing the years of fighting had taught every sane human being on Earth, it was that death came easily to those who fought fair against those who didn't.

Big Oaf was continuing, 'Maybe we could even work together on a couple of things, like those Germans. Maybe I'd even let you look that machine over after the next sleep. Say-y-y——'

'Yes?' Pendrake stared at him warily.

'Didn't you tell me those fellers that captured you said they had your wife a prisoner? How'd you like to spend a coupla weeks leadin' an expedition to see if you could rescue her?'

Pendrake felt a surge of hope. And then he saw that the other's small, shrewd eyes were contemplating him sharply, and the excitement puffed out of him. Eleanor had to be rescued, yes, but he couldn't see himself bringing her down here until he had consolidated his position with Devlin and the others. Couldn't see himself at all on an expedition of which the large purpose would be mass women-stealing.

Compromise, plus his own desperate necessity, was going to make for complications.

Seventeen

'It's time to get up!'

Morrison came into the bedroom the next morning with the announcement.

'Time?' Pendrake stared at the slim, young-looking man. 'Isn't all time down here the same? Why shouldn't I just stay here until I get hungry?'

To his surprise, Morrison shook his head doggedly. 'You've been sick, but that's over. Now you've got to fit into the routine. Big Oaf says so.'

Pendrake stared at the other's lean face. The thought in his mind was that Morrison was being used to spy on his activities. It had occurred to him before that this clerkish little fellow was a lackey of Big Oaf, but how much of a slave, was not clear. It struck him that his plan to spend the next few days in an intensive sizing up of everything and everybody in this strange land might as well begin here and now. Not that Morrison was dangerous as an individual. The man would always be a supporter of the regime that was in.

'Big Oaf,' Morrison answered his query, 'has got everything organized. Twelve hours for sleep, four hours for eating and so on—you don't have to eat or sleep, of course. You can do anything you want so long as you're ready to do your eight hours a day work.'

'Work?'

Morrison explained, 'There's guard duty; the cows have to be milked twice a day. Then there's the gardens to look after, and we kill several steers a week. It's all work.' He pointed with a sweep of his arm, vaguely. 'The gardens are over there beyond some trees, in the opposite direction from the pit where the beast is.' He finished, 'Big Oaf wants to know what you can do.'

Pendrake smiled wryly. So the apeman was letting him know what life would be like if he was not one of the bosses. It wasn't the work but the sudden vivid picture of the tight system of a law-and-order hierarchy behind it that was unsettling. Pendrake frowned, said finally, 'Tell Big

Oaf that I can milk cows, work in gardens, do guard duty, and a couple of other things.'

But there was no work orders for him that day. Or the next. He wandered around the town. Some of the men re-buffed his approaches; others were so uneasy that talking to them was a hopeless chore; still others, including men who were staunch supporters of Big Oaf, were curious about Earth. Some of them had the idea that he was going to be one of them.

In the course of the conversations, Pendrake learned the case histories of miners, gamblers, cowboys. His composite picture grew clearer. The main group of them belonged to a period between 1825 and 1875. He placed the trail where the transport machine was focused to be within twenty miles of an old frontier settlement called Canyon Town.

On the third morning Devlin crawled into Pendrake's bed-room just as he was getting up. 'I noticed Morrison going to the stockade,' the man said, 'so I sneaked over. We're ready, Pendrake.'

Pendrake jumped a little and then settled down onto the bed. He sat there grimly wondering what these men with their complete inexperience of a really planned war considered adequate readiness. He listened, trying to picture everything in scenes, as Devlin began :

'The central idea is to take the stockade and force sur-render. The men don't fancy a lot of bloodshed. The details are——'

Pendrake listened to the childish scheme, conscious of a great weariness. All his advice had been ignored. The ruth-less surprise attack that alone would make for a quick victory, bloodless for the attacker, had been shelved for a vague scheme to get the enemy cornered in the stockade, 'Listen, Devlin,' he said finally, 'look at me. For two days I've been doing nothing. You'd think I didn't have a care in the world. Yet my wife's in the hands of the damnedest, most murderous bunch of gangsters that ever lived on Earth. My country is in a danger that it doesn't even know about. Furthermore, three days ago Big Oaf asked me if I'd like to lead an attack against the Germans on the chance that they have my wife here on the moon. Why am I not rushing forward when I'm nearly crazy with anxiety? Because defeat is ten times as easy as victory, and more final. Because all the will in the world isn't enough if the strategy is bungled. As for bloodshed—you don't seem to realize you're dealing with a man who won't hesitate a second to order a general massacre if his position is ever threatened.

'And you don't seem to realize how skillfully this place is organized. The outward appearance is deceptive. Unless you work fast, you'll have all the doubtful men against you, and they'll fight twice as hard to prove to Big Oaf that they were with him all the time.

'Now, let's organize for battle, not a game. Tell me what's in those guarded buildings?'

'Guns in one of them, spears and bows and arrows in another, tools in a third—everything that ever came through from Earth, Big Oaf took possession of.'

'Where's the ammunition for the guns?'

'Only Big Oaf knows—— Say, I'm beginning to see what you mean. If he ever gets those guns going—— We've got to capture them.'

'If,' said Pendrake, 'the first arrow fired by every man could kill or disable one of them, our little war would be over in ten minutes, but——'

There was a scrambling sound at the doorway. Morrison crawled through. He was breathing hard, as if he had been running. 'Big Oaf,' he gasped, 'wants to show you the transport machine. Shall I tell him you're coming?'

There was no question of that. Pendrake went at once.

The transport machine stood inside a high timber stockade built at the edge of a cliff. It was made of a dark, almost drab metal, and its base was solid metal. Pausing on the wooden platform that ran around the upper edge of the stockade, Pendrake frowned down at the unbeautiful structure. In spite of all his will, he was excited, because if he could get this marvelous instrument to work, if he could focus it *anywhere*, say into the German prison where Eleanor was, or into American military headquarters or—— Or even if he could simply learn how to reverse it!

Shakily he forced the hope out of his mind. Thirty feet long, he estimated, twelve high and eighteen wide. Big enough for almost anything except a locomotive. He walked along the platform and paused finally where it twisted to the very edge of the precipice. The distance that stretched below shocked him. His body did not succumb easily to dizziness, but it wasn't necessary to take the risk merely to get a down look at the mouth of the machine.

He drew back. He faced Big Oaf, who had been sitting watching him with expressionless eyes. 'How do you get into the stockade?' Pendrake asked.

'There's a door at the other side.'

There was. Padlocked. Big Oaf fumbled down into the fur that was strapped around his great belly and produced a key. As the creature swung open the heavy door, Pendrake extended his hand.

'How about letting me have the lock? I don't think I could climb up those walls if I happened to get left inside.'

He spoke deliberately. He had done a lot of thinking of what his face-to-face policy with Big Oaf should be, and it seemed even now in the speaking that open distrust expressed without rancor was psychologically correct.

Big Oaf grimaced. 'That place ain't for you. I built it strong and high like that so nobody or nuthin' could come through from Earth and catch me by surprise.'

'Nevertheless,' Pendrake insisted, 'I wouldn't be able to concentrate properly if I had even the feeling that maybe——'

Big Oaf grunted. 'Look,' he said, 'maybe you'd like to lock me in.'

Pendrake pointed. 'See that hill over there, about a hundred yards?'

'Yeh?'

'Throw it over there.'

Big Oaf stared at him surlily, then he cursed. 'Like hell! Suppose somebody's over there to pick it up and lock us both in? Then they put an arrow in me an' let you out.'

In spite of his tenseness, Pendrake smiled. 'You're one ahead of me,' he confessed. He frowned finally. It wasn't that he had any real fear of Big Oaf at this stage. The man didn't have to use trickery, not yet. And it might be a good idea, now that his protest had been made, to let the beast-man win. Not too fast, though. 'Ever leave anybody in there?' he asked.

The squat man hesitated. 'Yeah,' he said. 'Two funny-lookin' guys all dressed up in metal. They had a damn queer gun, all kinds of fine wires on it, and the whole thing shining with a blue light. I used to have a scar on my shoulder where they burned me with it. I was scared stiff they'd burn down the stockade, but I guess it didn't work on wood.' He sighed hoarsely with regret. 'I'd sure like to have had that gun. But they took it with them when they jumped over the cliff.' Big Oaf explained, 'All this was long ago, maybe half the time I was here.'

Human beings with heat guns and metal suits five hundred thousand years ago—locked up with the machine for weeks. He tried to picture them caught in this towering horror of a cage, with an ape-thing looking down at them. The picture grew so vivid that for a moment he could almost *see* the men, staggering from thirst and hunger and insanity, leaping down to the merciful death below.

The vastness of the elapsed time—and a crowding thought —grew enormous. He said at last, wearily, 'You must be a sap, Big Oaf. If men who could make and understand guns like that couldn't make the machine reverse itself, how do you expect me to? In their desperation they must have tried everything.'

'Huh!' said Big Oaf. Then he cursed his comprehension of the defeat that was here.

Pendrake said, 'I'll have a look, anyway. '

The machine lay hard on the rock, an expanse of smooth metal with a deep indentation where it functioned. Pendrake walked in without much hope. He saw that the active wall was pierced with millions of tiny, needle-sized holes. It felt slightly warm to the touch. There were no knobs or dials or levers.

He was glancing around curiously when he realized that he already understood how the machine worked. It had come upon him so instantaneously but so gently that it was as if he had always known.

Space, time, and matter were products of chaotic motions which, by chance, had produced the universe in its present state. Science was a piecemeal attempt to bring order into a few of those chance motions.

This machine rectified *all* of the chance motions where it stood and wherever it connected to. Its very shape, including the cave-like indentation, was a condition of pure and perfect order as opposed to disorder. Because it totally eliminated the distortions of chance conglomeration, it had not only one purpose but could be converted (depending on what it was connected to) to any energy purpose whatsoever.

Nor was it really a matter transmitter between the moon and Earth. In an orderly space, this small area in the moon's interior belonged next to the small area on Earth along which the people and the animals had been traveling when they were so abruptly precipitated to a land of eternal life.

Since in perfect nature energy-flows followed exact rhythms and reversed at precise intervals, the two spaces were not always connected. The rhythm, as Pendrake perceived it with complete understanding, consisted of approximately ten minutes of flow from the Earth to the moon, followed by slightly more than eight hours of adjustment (an astonishing phenomenon in itself), then ten minutes of flow from the moon to the Earth, and again eight hours and a little bit for adjustment, whereupon the cycle repeated, beginning again with ten minutes of flow from the Earth to the moon.

It was only during the flow period that people could cross as if there were no distance. Depending on the direction of the flow, they could either go to Earth or come from Earth to the moon.

He perceived that several hours of adjustment had now passed and that several more hours must go by before the next flow from the moon to Earth would automatically enable anyone who walked in under the indentation to go to Earth.

All this was but one tiny function of the machine. Most of the other functions required a specific catalyst for each process to take place.

Pendrake turned and walked out of the metal 'cave,' and he had no doubt that he would have to tell Big Oaf that he knew how to operate the machine. He had status with this man only if he was useful to him. Quietly he said, 'I've figured out how this machine works. I can go to Earth or send someone if I have time to prepare—probably need a whole day to get the thing organized.'

The Neanderthal glowered at him suspiciously. 'Like you said, how come you could figger it and those fellers with the heat gun couldn't?'

Pendrake shrugged. 'Maybe they were just ordinary people of their civilization who could use things but didn't know how they worked.'

The monster was not so easily put off. 'Me and the other fellers just came through without preparations. Why should it take you time to get it ready?' he said.

It was a good question, but if Big Oaf ever found out the answer to that he wouldn't need Pendrake.

Pendrake said, 'That's why there's so few of you here. If you want me to, I'll set the machine so it'll pick up every person who comes along that trail.'

That was a lie, but since it was undoubtedly the last thing Big Oaf would want, it was a safe offer to make.

Big Oaf showed alarm. 'You ain't comin' near this place again.'

Pendrake hesitated, then changed the subject. 'Anybody ever escape from here?' he asked.

There was a long pause. 'One feller,' Big Oaf admitted finally, scowling. ''Bout a hunnert years ago. Lambton was his handle. He was an engineer surveyin' in the West for a railroad, he said. Smooth feller! Talked so good I let him look over the machines. He flew off in one of 'em up a cave. I closed that tunnel off, you can betcha, but I was sure uneasy for a long time. Finally figgered he couldn't have made it to Earth, and so I began to feel better.'

Pendrake heard the final comments only vaguely, because with the mention of the name Lambton this entire patchwork of events that had involved him so thoroughly suddenly made sense. A tiny artifact—the engine—of an ancient lunar civilization had found its way to Earth. Apparently that earlier Lambton had done nothing with it. But not too many years ago the son or grandson of the man known to Big Oaf had evidently interested a group of idealists—scientists, businessmen, and professional people—in the engine as a means for peacefully settling the planets. Where the engine had been all the years since it had been taken from the moon needed to be explained. But one thing was dismally clear. A large percentage of the group that had become associated with it were now either murdered or in prison, and the survivors were probably much wiser about the severity of the problem of bringing peace to a planet inhabited by hostile people. Since most idealists were themselves extremely angry people, the whole thing was a sorry mess, indeed.

Standing there, he judged that civilization would evolve at its own slow pace and that even highly educated, well-meaning people could not speed that pace except perhaps infinitesimally.

Pendrake said diplomatically, 'You said there were other machines ...' He left the question hanging.

His answer was a scowl and a harsh 'You ain't seein' no other machines till we make a deal. And just in case you figger you got lots of time to lie around here gettin' all set with Devlin to knock me off my perch—that last expedition is leavin' tomorrow for some more women. I'm not even waitin' for t'other to get back.'

Pendrake was silent. For a man with as much knowledge as he now had, he was singularly powerless to act. The next flow of energy from the moon to Earth was still hours away.

And he had none of the catalysts to stimulate those other equally potent functions of the machine.

Big Oaf was continuing, 'I wasn't gonna send it till t'other one got back, but I gotta hunch it's time we start pullin' down the caves between us and them Germans. You can go or not, any way it suits your play, but you better make up your mind fast. Now come on, let's get back to town.'

There was silence between them as they walked. Pendrake's mind was seething. So Big Oaf was forcing issues, taking no chances. He studied the waddling creature out of the corners of his eyes, trying to read in the heavy, brutish countenance something of the purpose behind it. But impassivity was the natural state of the facial structure. Only the implacable physical strength of the man stabbed forth in every movement, every writhing muscle.

Pendrake said finally, 'How do you get up to the surface? There's no air or warmth up there, is there?' He added before Big Oaf could speak: 'What kind of quarters have the Germans made for themselves?'

A minute dragged. It began to seem as if the apeman would not reply. But abruptly he grunted, 'It's the lighted passages that's warm and got air in them. A whole bunch of 'em run right to the surface, some of 'em hidden damn smart by doors that look like rock or dirt. That's how we fooled the Germans so far. We just rush out of a new door and——'

A shout cut off his words. A man burst over the near hill and ran toward them. Pendrake recognized him as a Big Oaf hanger-on. The fellow came up, breathing hard. 'They're back with the women. The men are going wild.'

'They'd better watch out!' Big Oaf growled. 'They know what they'll get if they touch any of 'em before I see 'em.'

There were about thirty women huddled in the open land before the apeman's stockade. The motley throng of men gathered around them set up a wild yelling as Big Oaf and Pendrake came into view. Lusting voices squealed with demand and counterdemand.

'I've got only one wife; I got a right to another.' 'It's my turn.' 'Big Oaf, you gotta——' 'I've earned——'

'*Shurrup!*'

The silence was instantaneous and almost deafening and was broken finally by a bull-necked man who came up to Big Oaf and said, 'I guess that's the last women rustlin' we do, boss. Those blankety-blank Germans were ready for us, and they seemed to have explored all the cave approaches to their place. They followed us like a bunch of vigilantes, and we escaped only by knocking down that narrow cutoff at——'

'I know the one. How many fellers dead?'

'Twenty-seven.'

Big Oaf was silent for a long moment, frowning. Finally he said, 'Well, let's get t'the pickin'. I'm taking one for myself, and——'

'*Jim!*'

Pendrake had been listening grimly to the conversation. Now he spun on his heel and stared wildly at a lithely built young woman who was running toward him, crying as she ran. She flung herself into his enfolding arms and lay against him in a half faint.

Over her limp, dark head Pendrake gazed straight into Big Oaf's grinning face. 'Somebody you know?' the monster smirked.

'My wife!' Pendrake said, and there was a terrible sinking sensation in him. He found himself looking around for Devlin, but the man didn't seem to be in the crowd. Swallowing hard, he faced forward again.

Big Oaf's grin was so wide now, it showed all the great husks of his teeth. Still grinning, he said slyly, 'My play is, you take her, Pendrake. Get the feel of having her again, and then, maybe in a week—hey!—we can talk.'

It was reprieve. For two days Pendrake felt a desperate, angry relief. Relief that he had been given a little time. Anger that he could do virtually nothing to stop the degradation of the other women. He told one of Devlin's subleaders to spread the rumor that any man who took one of the new women would suffer severe consequences. But that only increased his desperation, for the rumor, to be effective, had to include his name as the avenging individual He presumed anxiously that the story would come to Big Oaf's ears, and that grim personality would quite correctly analyze that Pendrake was threatening his authority.

Pendrake kept all his doorways blocked during the sleep period. And Eleanor and he talked far into each 'night.' At first she was very dramatic. 'You can depend on it,' she said fiercely, 'that I shall kill myself instantly if that creature or anyone here but you ever tries to touch me. I belong only to you.'

It was a woman talking to her man, and Pendrake listened uneasily, for he had no solution either.

On the third day Devlin came to see him. The lean man stood in the doorway and stared at Pendrake, a saturnine expression on his face. 'Well,' he said, 'so now you can feel in your own innards what standin' up to Big Oaf may mean. Shall we call off the feud and eat crow for His Majesty?'

Pendrake shook his head. 'I've been thinking,' he said slowly. 'There's a way in which we can divide this place up into areas, one that we control and one that we leave to Big Oaf and his henchmen.'

He inclined his head toward the door, and they crawled outside. Pendrake leading the way, they walked to a nearby height. He indicated the vista below: the rest of the town, the meadows, and the beautiful valley beyond.

'There're several water sources. If we can take those on that side'—he pointed—'we can always, if pressed, fall back to the caves, escape up toward the surface, and contact the Germans as a last defense . . .'

He left the sentence unfinished. The Germans offered them no haven at all, of course, but these men wouldn't clearly understand what remorseless characters they were.

'By heaven,' said Devlin, 'maybe you've got a

thought——' He broke off. 'But you're changin' your tune. Now it's no longer a fight to the finish.'

'If we get half,' Pendrake acknowledged.

Devlin was nodding thoughtfully. 'Half the cattle, half the guns . . .'

'We set up a democracy in our half,' said Pendrake, 'and we fight to defend it, but we don't cross the border. Presently they'll get the idea.'

The lean man was silent. 'How're you going to do it?' he demanded abruptly.

'Tell your most trusted people,' said Pendrake. 'We'll act before the week is out. There's no alternative.'

Devlin held out his hand. They shook hands and separated, the tall man going down one side of the height and Pendrake another side. As Pendrake came back to his house he saw that, brief as his absence had been, he had a visitor.

Big Oaf squatted just outside the low doorway.

The monster grinned at him in a genial fashion. 'Thought I'd pay me respects,' he said, 'an' maybe have one more talk, hey?'

Pendrake studied the other with wary respect. It struck him that he had never before in his life confronted an adversary at once so dangerous and intelligent. He did not doubt that he was about to receive final warning.

Big Oaf said, 'Pendrake, I been learnin' about women.'

Pendrake stiffened.

The creature stared at him, suddenly sober. 'I get the feelin' me havin' those women bothers you.'

That was putting it mildly. Pendrake cringed inwardly whenever he thought of it. He said now, 'Where I come from, a woman chooses the man she marries.'

Big Oaf pursed his lips and put up a hand as if rejecting the argument. 'Aw, come, now—you know I'd never get a one by choice. Those females would pick a nuthin' like Miller before they'd choose me. Ain't that so?'

Pendrake agreed that it was so. But it occurred to him that he could not discuss this subject objectively. He had too much emotion tied up in the male–female relationship. It amazed him to realize how strong the feeling was, but his taut, hostile attitude did not let go.

'Pendrake—know something? Three of those dames are

beginnin' to fight over me. Whaddya make o' that?' Big Oaf shook his hideous head, puzzled but obviously pleased. 'Women ain't put together the same as men, Pendrake. If you'd'a asked me when I first picked 'em, I'd'a sworn on a stack of Bibles nary a one would give me a tumble. But I played it smart. No kissin'. Y'understand. I wanted to nuzzle 'em, believe me, but I figgered a woman havin' me pushin' my face into hers would—well, you know, two of those females killed themselves. That gave me a shock. I sure didn't want that to happen again, so there's been no more kissin'.'

'What about the other three women?' Pendrake asked.

Big Oaf scowled. He sat on his haunches for at least a minute, all the geniality gone from him. The glare faded out of his eyes, and he relaxed visibly. 'Things like this take time, Pendrake,' he explained carefully. 'I'm tellin' you what I'm learnin' about women. The way I figger it, a woman has got to have some man. If she can't have a good man, she'll have a bad one. If she can't have a good-lookin' one, she'll take an ugly one. Nature made her that way, and she can't help it. In most ways she can think as good as a man, but not about that. . . . Those other three women. Wanta know how I handle 'em? First I start 'em learnin' English. Got a feller here who speaks German, and I use him as interpreter. I have him tell 'em people stay alive here forever. That makes 'em think. Same time, I have him tell 'em that I'm the boss in this here place. Women like to be with the boss. Then, soon as they've learned some words, I make it clear I'm a pretty gentle type if you don't cross me. I tell ya, Pendrake, it's gonna work. Well, whaddya think?'

It was a bid for friendship. This half animal really wanted the good will of his principal potential opponent. Pendrake shook his head finally. 'Big Oaf,' he said, 'free all six of those women. Order your henchmen to free theirs. If three of those wives of yours are really fighting over you, then one of them will stay with you as your permanent wife. If all the women are freed, I predict the men can start courting right away, and they'll be surprised to find that after the women get over the initial shock of being here at all they'll look the men over as prospective husbands. It won't be long before marriages take place.'

The Neanderthal stood up. 'That's all you got to say?' He glowered.

'You know in your heart I'm talking truth,' said Pendrake in a steady voice.

'You're talkin' yourself into trouble,' was the harsh reply. 'I ain't just havin' one woman, and I'm runnin' this here town.'

Pendrake said nothing, simply stood there. Big Oaf scowled at him and then with a snarling sound whirled and lumbered off.

Pendrake knelt and crawled into the house. He found Eleanor on the other side of the door anxiously waiting.

'What do you think he'll do?' she asked.

Pendrake shook his head. 'I don't know,' he confessed.

But the hollow feeling in the pit of his stomach told him that the die was cast.

Nineteen

Devlin reported the following day that he had told his four
subleaders and that they also felt that the issue must be
forced. They had expressed themselves—so Devlin said—as
being pleased with the compromise plan. They welcomed
the idea of two communities. Hearing this, Pendrake had
the thought that the men were probably happy for the
wrong reason : out of weakness rather than strength. But
the important thing was that they accepted the idea. He
realized he also was glad that perhaps total war could be
avoided.

The plan Devlin and he agreed upon was simple. They
would seize half the water sources, and those of the cattle
tenders who were Devlin's men would drive half the herd
over toward the caves. They would seize two of the four
stockades, the one with the bows and arrows and the one
with the guns. This would leave the hidden ammunition and
undoubtedly a few rifles and revolvers in Big Oaf's possession. Pendrake felt that such a small quantity of guns could
be balanced by showers of arrows particularly in the close
confinement of the town itself.

Guards would be stationed at key points, and mobile
groups of men would be kept on the alert, ready to rush to
the aid of guards at any key point that was attacked.

Devlin agreed that it was the best plan, but he perspired
profusely as he admitted it. 'This is the toughest deal I've
ever been in,' he confessed, 'but I'll have this all figgered and
the men assigned in a day or two, and I'll let you know.'

With that he departed.

The next day went by without any words.

The following morning Morrison knocked at the door. He
announced, 'Big Oaf says half of each group is to come to
the place in front of his stockade. He says for me to tell you
he wants you there and that he knows somethin' is up, and
he wants to head it off by makin' peace before there's any
fight. Women's to come as well as men. Meetin's in one
hour.'

Pendrake with Eleanor on his arm walked to the 'meetin'.'

He was uneasy, and as he approached he was relieved to see that a number of Devlin's men and their women were approaching. He drew a Devlin subleader aside and said, 'Send word to Devlin to get his forces together and just stand by.'

The man replied, 'Devlin's already doin' that, so I guess things are in order.'

Pendrake was even more relieved. For that meant all possible was being done. For the first time the thought came that perhaps this would work out after all without bloodshed.

In front of the stockade the crowd swelled until well over two hundred men and almost three hundred women were gathered. Most of the German girls were on the good-looking side. There was no question that this gang of Old West settlers had acquired a rare collection of attractive females, that with such prizes at stake everyone was in deadly earnest, and that Big Oaf's peace plan would have to be good to give each man a feeling of security.

Near the entrance to the stockade there was a stir. The big gate opened, and a moment later the Neanderthal waddled forth. The semi-man climbed onto a small platform and looked around. His gaze lighted on Pendrake. He pointed with his finger. 'H'you, Pendrake!' he roared.

It must have been a signal, for there was a scream from Eleanor. 'Jim—watch out!'

The next instant something hard hit his head, and he felt himself falling.

Blackness.

When Pendrake came to, Devlin was anxiously bending over him. Most of the people were gone. The tall man was rueful. 'We were fools,' he said. 'He grabbed your wife, and he's got her in there now. I guess he figgered you're the leader of any rebellion, and if he can stop you he can stop the rest of us.' He added shamefacedly, 'Maybe he can.'

Pendrake sat up with a groan.

Then he stood up, and rage surged. He snapped, 'How long will it take to get the attack started?'

Devlin produced a whistle. 'I blow twice on this,' he said, 'and in five minutes we're started.'

'I see.' Pendrake was recovering rapidly, and his eyes were

narrowed in calculation. Then : 'Blow the whistle,' he said, 'as soon as I'm inside the stockade.'

Devlin swallowed, and some of the color faded from his cheeks. 'I guess this is it,' he muttered. He drew a knife from an inside pocket. 'Here, take this.'

Pendrake took it and slipped it into his pocket.

Devlin had another thought. 'How you gonna get in?' he asked.

'Don't worry about that,' Pendrake flung over his shoulder. To the guards he said, 'Tell Big Oaf that I'm ready to talk business.'

Big Oaf crawled grinning out of the house inside the stockade. 'I thought you'd see sense,' he said, and then grunted as the knife Pendrake threw buried itself seven inches in his great chest.

He tore the bloody thing out of his flesh and, grimacing, flung it to the ground. "You get the pit for that,' he said. 'I'll just tie you up and——'

He came forward and a chill raced up Pendrake's back. The monster's head was bent low. His animal arms were spread out. The abnormal strength of the man showed in all its hideous power. Watching the creature waddle toward him, Pendrake was suddenly stunned by the thought that no man born in the last hundred thousand years could begin to have the superhuman strength necessary to defeat this hairy, titanic beast.

Pendrake backed away warily. His first horror of the muscled collosus that was lumbering toward him faded. But the conviction that he must wait for a favorable opening was an ugly surging along his nerves, a high, sustained thrill unlike anything he had ever known. Unashamed of his reluctance, yet desperate in the need for haste, he waited for the attack that Devlin and his men were to launch—anything that would distract the beast's attention.

When the attack came with an abrupt roaring of men's voices, Pendrake flung himself forward, straight at the hairy man. A bearlike arm reached out to grab him. He knocked it aside and for a fleeting second had his opportunity. The blow he leveled against that massive jaw nearly broke his fist. Even then all would have been well if the smash had accomplished its purpose. It didn't. The monster, instead of staggering for that instant of leeway that Pendrake had counted on to get away, plunged forward. His cable-thick arms closed around Pendrake's shoulders.

The Neanderthal bellowed with triumph. As the creature started his terrible squeeze, Pendrake jerked free his imprisoned arms, jabbed two fingers at Big Oaf's pig eyes, shoved hard—and tore his body from that deadly embrace.

It was his turn to cry out with the wild glee of a man in the full grip of battle lust: 'You're licked, Big Oaf! You're through. You——'

With a hoarse cry the hairy man leaped towards him. Laughing harshly, Pendrake danced back. Too late, he noticed the throne platform directly behind. His retreat, made easy by the moon's gravity, was too swift for sudden halt. With a crash he fell flat on his back on the platform.

It was over as swiftly as that. On his feet he might have won; in that one test of strength he had not been entirely outmatched. But Big Oaf kneeling on top of him, striking at him with body-breaking fists, was another story. In a minute Pendrake was clinging to his senses by the barest thread of consciousness. He was only dimly aware of being roughly and abruptly tied.

Slowly his mind crept farther out of the darkness, into fuller comprehension of the disaster that had befallen him. He said finally, thickly, 'You fool! Do you hear that fighting out there? It means you're through, no matter what you do to me. Better make a deal, Big Oaf, while there's still a chance.'

One look into those creature eyes brought the sick knowledge that he had flung his tiny stone of hope into a shadowed world. All the beast in the man was to the fore. The enormous lips were drawn back; teeth protruded like fangs; Big Oaf snarled with little grunts of fury; he said finally with a guttural hoarseness, 'I'll just bar the gate from this side. That'll make my men fight harder 'cause they won't be able to retreat in here. And it'll make sure that you and me have our little show all to ourselves.'

He lumbered massively out of Pendrake's line of vision. There was the sound of timber crashing into position. Then the hairy thing came into sight again, grinning now. But when he spoke it was like a carnivore spitting rage: 'I'm gonna live here a million years, Pendrake, 'n' all that time your wife's gonna be one of my women.'

Pendrake gritted, 'You mad idiot, even if you win now, you'll die fast enough when the Germans come. And don't think they won't, either. You're just a bunch of bandits to them, a nuisance that they won't put up with for very long.'

The words seemed not to touch the mind of the other. The man was, astonishingly, tugging at the throne platform. Pendrake watched, puzzled, as Big Oaf strained with all his enormous strength at the wooden thing.

Abruptly the structure lifted. It came up and reeled over with a crash as Big Oaf flung it away from him. Where its timbered sides had been lay the entrance to a cave. 'Those fools,' Big Oaf said with withering contempt, 'thought I had this platform here, and this stockade, because I wanted to play king. The blue men know the truth, but they won't learn any language but their own, so they can't tell even if they want to, which they don't.'

He was bending over Pendrake as he finished. With a grunt he heaved him to his shoulder and jumped down into the lighted cave.

It was a twenty-foot drop. At the bottom he tossed his prisoner unceremoniously to the cave floor and climbed back to the surface. 'Don't get anxious,' he called back mockingly. 'I'm just gonna let the platform down into place.'

He landed with a thud a minute later and picked Pendrake up again. 'This cave,' he said then, grinning, 'leads straight to the pit. I'm gonna lower you down to my ole pal, the devil-beast, and watch the fun. It'll be some fun, feller, uh !'

The cave sloped gently downward and presently began to widen. It opened abruptly into a huge room filled with metal shapes.

Machines! They shone in the reflected light of the cave walls and ceilings. They stood there, silent, secret witnesses to the glory of a people who had attained—not quite immortality, for they were dead—but a measure of greatness probably unequaled in the solar system before or since.

At a point where two corridors divided, Big Oaf paused. He stood for a long moment and then deliberately lowered Pendrake to the hard flooring. He knelt silently and with thick, clumsy fingers unloosed the bonds around Pendrake's ankles.

'Get up!' he commanded curtly.

That, with the moon's gravity, was no problem at all, even though his hands were tied behind his back, cruelly tight. 'Down the right tunnel!' Big Oaf ordered.

As Pendrake obeyed without a word, the Neanderthal followed and presently said, 'There's suthin' down here I want you to see. Always gives me a queer feeling, and it'd be kind of nutty of me t' kill you without askin' a guy like you what it does to you.'

The radiant walls lighted their way, and they came to a large room. In the exact center of this room reared a limpidly transparent cube about twenty feet in diameter. Big Oaf motioned to it, and Pendrake walked over, aware of the creature puffing along behind him.

'Look down!' said the other, and his voice was almost gentle.

Pendrake had already seen.

At some depth below, a blue-white flame glowed with an intense brightness. After one glance Pendrake had to look away. But he kept looking at it with quick additional glances.

'It's been shiny like that,' said Big Oaf, 'since I came here. What do you make of it, feller?'

Pendrake said silently, agonizingly, into the cube, 'Please

rescue me. I need help!'

From some vast distance in the cube a voice answered into his brain, 'Friend, your ability to sense our presence gains you nothing, for it will be long indeed before men can use what we have and know.'

'Have mercy,' Pendrake said shakily. 'I am about to be murdered by a wild animal and eaten.'

'Very well, you may choose. Join us in here forever.'

'You mean——'

'Forever absorbed into the unity, free of all passion and pain forever.'

Pendrake shrank. His instantaneous reaction was total revulsion. He had no feeling at all that he was being offered freedom. For that instant terror of the sabertooth vanished, because the alternative sounded like a living hell.

'But my wife, Earth, all these people,' Pendrake protested shakily. 'There's terrible danger . . .'

The voice in his mind said, 'Decide before you leave this room. We can help you here. We cannot help you . . . outside . . .'

'You are the moon people?' he asked distractedly.

'We are the moon people.'

Trembling, Pendrake turned from the cube to face his captor. 'Big Oaf,' he said tensely, 'with my wife here, you can make me do anything you want. Surely, the last thing you should do with a man who must obey you is to kill him.'

'You're too smart. I don't trust you!' the creature snarled. 'I don't get a feeling that you'll deal.'

'I've got to deal,' urged Pendrake. 'I have no choice.'

'You're too much of a man for me to have around,' the creature argued. 'Nobody's ever been able to stand up to me before.'

Pendrake said flatly, 'So long as my wife's here, you've got me.'

'It didn't stop you from attacking me.'

'I was kind of crazy-mad from that blow on the head,' said Pendrake, 'and I wasn't thinking straight.'

Big Oaf seemed to consider that, mouth open, eyes half closed. Abruptly his teeth snapped shut. 'To hell with that!' he snarled. 'I ain't takin' no chances. Since you've been here there's been trouble, and so I'm gonna get rid of all these troublemakers, startin' with you. I got a long time, Pendrake, to get my other problems straightened. Now, get goin'.'

Pendrake went, slowly. He said nothing more to the life essence whose presence he had detected in the flame. He had no further thought of what they had offered as being a solution for him. Their existence was beyond his reality. Up the corridor they went, and soon there were more machines.

'I'm takin' you this way,' Big Oaf taunted, 'to show you what you could have had. And you could have had your wife. But now I'll wait until some other guy comes along who knows about machines and ain't so fussy. Maybe I'll give your wife to him, too,' he added as an afterthought, and bellowed with laughter.

Pendrake remained silent. But his mind was rocking back and forth like a swing swaying higher and more wildly with each surge. And every minute the load on that careening brain grew heavier. There was the engine, an Earth that did not suspect what the East Germans were doing; there was Eleanor . . .

The thought ended as if it had been cut out of his brain with a knife. The blood drained from his cheeks. The muscles of his solar plexus drew so tight that it was like an acute appendix pain. For Big Oaf and he had come again to the stockade which contained the Earth transport machine. As Pendrake watched with sick eyes, the monster-man unlocked the padlock and swung the gate open. 'Get in there!' Big Oaf snarled.

Pendrake, who had been vainly tugging at his bonds as they walked, stepped forward rapidly. 'One more chance,' he thought, and only speed and absolute disregard for pain made it a chance at all.

As he passed the gate he stopped for an instant, bent forward, put his arms way up behind him, and hooked them onto an out-jut of stockade. With all his strength and all the power of his legs, he jerked forward.

He had earlier felt the dry age of the rope. And now it ripped like thick, old grass.

And he was free.

Slightly off balance, he whirled. Then he lunged at the gate.

It clicked shut in his face, and there was a metallic clank as the padlock locked tight.

Big Oaf's voice came from beyond the gate. 'Ye're a pretty smart feller, Pendrake. Too smart for me to take any chances. I ain't waitin' till you get that machine workin'. I'm gettin' me a rifle, and I'll be back to pot you in there in less'n thirty minutes.'

There was a sound of footsteps receding, crunching, fading.

It was not, Pendrake thought shakily, a really good day for either Big Oaf or himself.

He had already sensed that the flow to Earth was due in a little over fifteen minutes. Reluctant as he was to leave, he obviously had no alternative. Anxiously he waited for the fifteen-minute period to pass.

He thought in agony, 'Oh, God, Eleanor is in his hands!'

And still there was no alternative to leaving.

He thought hopelessly, 'They'll think Big Oaf fed me to the devil-beast, and they'll knuckle under.'

He visualized Eleanor's grief and degradation, and he thought, 'I've got to go, get equipment and weapons, and come back, all in eight hours.'

That would set a time limit on the damage and humiliation the monster could inflict.

Big Oaf might even hold off doing anything to Eleanor for fear that Pendrake would be back. It was his only real hope for her safety.

No alternative.

As the flow began, Pendrake reluctantly walked to the invisible dividing line under the cave-like indentation, stopped, spread his legs to gain a firm footing, and then he bent forward and poked his head and shoulders through. He wanted a good clear look at what was on the other side.

Darkness. No. Rather, a kind of foggy nothingness.

Pendrake pulled back, nonplused. Could it be night on Earth? Undoubtedly it could be. Yet nights were seldom *that* dark. Dissatisfied, he bent forward once more.

It was like putting his head into a sack. Nothing was visible.

But he felt ever so slightly dizzy as he pulled back a second time.

Even more disturbing, he sensed that the seconds were rushing by and that ten minutes was a woefully short time for the precautions he ought to be taking.

Swiftly he walked over to one wall of the indentation, balanced himself, and then gingerly he poked his right leg through. His probing foot contacted only empty air.

Pendrake drew back, moved over several inches, and tried again. It was an eerie sensation to see his leg disappear, but far more disturbing when once more there was nothing but emptiness.

He estimated that it took altogether five minutes to inch along from one side of the machine to the other—and not once did his foot touch anything solid on the other side.

No alternative.

Pendrake thought almost blankly, 'Is it possible I'm going to have to take the gamble of jumping through?'

At least a minute raced by as he stood there in awful indecision. And finally there was no doubt about it.

Any instant Big Oaf would be back.

He thought hopefully, 'There's a trail. Everybody reports that. It's in the hills, but it's on relatively level ground. So if I jump and have my body relaxed, ready to give, so that I don't land hard ...'

As Pendrake leaped through, he had a kaleidoscope of impressions. A sheer wall of dirt reared up in front of him. He struck it with his face and body and started to slide down a steep incline. Simultaneously he was aware of the roar of a tractor. As he looked back he saw with horror that he was sliding down into the pathway of a huge road-roller machine. Pendrake yelled at the driver, but the man was staring to one side, guiding his monstrous instrument over some exactly measured route.

One yell of warning was all Pendrake had time to utter. The next instant he landed in front of the machine. With all his will he tried to thrust himself out of the path of the roller. Almost, he made it. Almost ...

Twenty-one

At odd moments throughout the day Jefferson Dayles studied the report of the scientists. The momentary perusals left him blankly puzzled. Later, when the sheer hard work of the presidential day was finally over, he took the report to bed with him and in the middle of the night reread the astonishing document. It was as follows:

'In the matter of the three engines seized by your agents when the Pendrake estate was taken over—there is no adequate way to describe these perfect machines. They seem to be a final-stage development of a new principle. The motive power appears to derive from the shape and construction of the doughnut-style metal tube. When taken apart, this tube proved to be put together by an advanced metallurgical technique and defies analysis in spite of our careful notation of each phase of the breakdown. The suggestion has been made that the tube was drawing power from a distant power broadcasting station, but this cannot be established. It is certainly not an atomic engine. There is no sign of radioactivity.

'As the same failure resulted when we took apart a second engine, we have determined not to dismantle the third and last engine until after a further study of the parts of the two engines already dismantled is made, perhaps by other personnel.

'It is possible the secret of their reaction may lie in some subtle alloy combination of the construction materials. Even the welding compound must be examined and analyzed for its influence. . . .

'The surpassing importance of cautious development can best be gauged by the fact that the power has other potentialities about which a report is being prepared. . . .'

Jefferson Dayles lay in the darkness with closed eyes. To him it seemed like the old, old story: too complicated for most mortal minds.

As he finally turned over to go to sleep, he thought: Three

years, and no more. Three years to find Pendrake. After that it might be too late.

Even as it was, he must first win the most fantastic election in the history of America.

Women were on the rampage. They had a candidate for the presidency, and it was almost as if this unhinged the minds of millions of formerly sensible females.

The candidate, a strong, clear-thinking feminine woman, balanced herself on the edge of the abyss and did her best to keep from falling in. She seemed to be aware of all the pitfalls, and though Dayles's agents kept a complete check on every statement and speech that she made in public, the months went by and she did not slip, and she did not fall.

Dayles observed the performance from a distance, at first with disbelief and then with admiration, but finally with alarm. 'She's got to get tired,' he said. 'One of these days she'll be so exhausted she can scarcely stand, and that's the moment for our people to trip her up.'

Whatever could be said about the rationality of the candidate did not apply to her followers. The millennium was about to arrive. Women could end war, bring peace to the troubled world. They would right the wrongs of society, control the rapaciousness of business, and once and for all they would end the infidelity of the American male.

Most of these ideas, of course, did not reach the level of actual public discussion.

A month before the voters were due to go to the polls, the President still confronted the stark reality that he might not win at all. From everywhere, from all his people—from the political machines, from local party bosses, from private and public polls—the word was the same: the woman candidate was ahead.

'We need a lucky break,' he said to Kay one hot day between speeches. 'I sense that my talks are not getting through the emotion stirred up in favor of Wake.' He always called his opponent Wake, not Mrs. Wake, not Janet Wake—just Wake. The technique of using only her last name emphasized equality in a fight where, for the first time in political history, the man was handicapped by the mere fact that he was a male.

Kay said coldly, 'Just in case the break doesn't come, I can tell you that all necessary steps have been taken to start a thousand riots, so that you can declare a national emergency and cancel the election.'

'Good,' said President Dayles, but beads of perspiration glistened on his forehead and cheeks. He took out his handkerchief. 'I'm fully determined,' Kay,' he said, 'so don't worry about my weakening. This woman issue is nothing more than one more insanity in a world that is confused by too many side issues already.'

The campaign grew hotter. Parades. Vast meetings. Women screaming slogans: Peace! Happy Homes! A Healthy Nation!

How would it all be accomplished? There were rumors of lashings for men who left their families. Deserted wives and mothers, properly feeling quite vengeful, embarrassed the great woman who was their candidate by urging that wife deserters should be whipped back into the home. Of what value they would be to their wives with their hearts filled with anger and their backs covered with the welts of the lash was never clearly defined. And it was openly stated by some women that one of the things these husbands wouldn't or shouldn't get was satisfaction for their lusts.

Two weeks before the election, at the end of an evening when Mrs. Wake was speaking to a throng of thousands, a woman got to a microphone and screamed a question: Did or did not the candidate support corporal punishment for males who deserted their families?

'Girls, girls,' said Mrs. Wake wearily, 'don't get ahead of yourselves!'

It was *the* unfortunate remark.

The Dayles press picked up the sentence.

The next day, and for many days thereafter, Wake tried to explain that she was merely trying to restrain the extremists.

But the honeymoon was over. Millions of men who had trusted her implicitly did a reversal. Suddenly her every word was no longer the epitome of good sense, but rather she was a sly female playing a game one step at a time.

It was reported that women also began to have doubts about a woman president. The easy, age-old hatred of women for other women, suspended in the intense emotional atmosphere of the campaign, suddenly reasserted itself.

The tide turned noticeably.

With inward relief President Dayles abandoned his plan to cancel the election.

As he stated in a speech a week before polling day: 'I confidently call on the electorate, women and men, to vote on the issues, to vote on the record of my administration.'

He was now so certain of victory that he could utter such stereotypes as if they were new and original with him.

He retired early and was awakened at midnight by Kay with the news report from Los Angeles: A long line of women had been marching with placards printed with such slogans as: HURRAH FOR THE RIGHTS OF WOMEN! PHYSICAL WORK FOR MEN, ADMINISTRATIVE FOR WOMEN! A JUST ORDERLY PEACEFUL WORLD, ADMINISTERED BY WOMEN.

Then—so the report said—had come a man's interrupting shout: 'Break it up; let's break it up! They're counting on us to respect them, while they make slaves of us. Come on!'

Men had surged sullenly from the sidelines and become a mob. When armored cars finally cleared the streets, twenty-four women lay dead, ninety-seven others were seriously injured, and more than four hundred required hospital treatment.

It was a crisis of the kind that could win or lose an election. At 12.30 a.m. President Dayles was on the air promising a thorough investigation and prompt punishment of the guilty.

It appeared that thirty-two men had been arrested. They were arraigned the next day. All had attorneys; all pleaded not guilty. The judge questioned each man briefly, and then, in an unprecedented judgment, pronounced that fifteen of the men were indeed not guilty but that the other seventeen were.

Whereupon he sentenced the seventeen to death.

The court was immediately in commotion, and it took a hundred special deputies to clear it and to separate the hysterical condemned from their stunned families and attorneys.

Later the judge calmly defended his action. 'It's perfectly in order for a judge to decide whether a man is guilty or not guilty. It must not be thought that democracies are too weak to deal with riots.'

He thereupon departed on a vacation, which—it was said —would take him and his family on an extended tour abroad.

Asked to comment on the judgment, Wake said uneasily, 'There is no doubt that justice has been done. I have asked a committee to look into the actual trial procedure and bring me a report.'

Dayles said, 'This is entirely a matter for the court system, which, as you all know, is a branch of government in the United States separate from the administrative.'

It was announced that the condemned men planned to appeal their sentence. On this note of suspense the election took place.

Jefferson Dayles was re-elected by a two-million majority.

He was greatly relieved, but, as he pointed out to Kay afterward, 'That's it! At the end of this term my legal right to be President runs out. Any continuation depends on——'

'Pendrake,' she finished for him.

'Pendrake,' he agreed somberly. He shook his head in a blank wonderment. 'What in the world could have happened to that man? I've had the FBI, army intelligence, and police everywhere looking for him. Not a sign.'

She said matter-of-factly, 'You've still got a few years.'

'Three.' He nodded. 'In three years I've got to make up my mind. After that it will probably be too late.'

Twenty-two

Inauguration . . .

Too late, too late . . . All that great day the words trampled through his mind, dulling his smiles, dimming his exultation, darkening all his thoughts. Find Pendrake! Find the man whose blood could in one week strip the old age from his body, and, in so doing, immortalize his power and the mighty civilization he visualized.

The thought was like a sickness, a craving, that was still upon him months later when they brought in the farmer. The man was big and rangy. As he sat listening to the fellow's colloquial account, one question quivered in Jefferson Dayles's mind. The problem of how to phrase it engaged his attention as the farmer's voice twanged on.

'Like I was sayin', he was at my place ten days, an' old Doc Gillespie came twice to look at him, but he didn't seem to need no medical attention, only food. Mind you, he did act queer. Couldn't seem to tell me his name or nothin'. Anyways, after his leg got well I took him to Carness and turned him over to the employment commission. I told them his name was Bill Smith. He didn't argue none about that, so that's what they put him down as—Bill Smith. They sent him out on some labor job, can't recollect just what it was. Anything else you want to know?'

Jefferson Dayles sat cold. But that was an outward covering for an inner excitement. Pendrake was alive, discovered, so Kay had reported, when the Carness police department belatedly sent Bill Smith's fingerprints to Washington.

'That's all we could find,' Kay had said. 'But at least we've got a place to start.'

'Yes,' Jefferson Dayles had replied and he had drawn a deep breath. 'Yes.'

The toti-potent man was alive.

There was one question that remained, a verification: Pendrake's arm! The one that had been regrowing.

The farmer's voice came again: 'There's one more thing, Mr. President——'

Jefferson Dayles waited, involved in the preparation of his

question. It was a hard sentence to utter because—well, how could you ask if a human being's arm had regrown? You couldn't, although the very idea was fascinating and mind-staggering.

'The thing,' said the farmer, 'is this: When I picked him up, I coulda swore one of his legs was shorter'n the other. But when he left, they was the same length. Now, am I crazy or——'

'Doesn't make much sense, does it?' said Jefferson Dayles. He went on quickly, 'He was otherwise all right, was he?'

The farmer nodded. 'Strongest man I ever saw. I tell you, when he lifted that wagon with those two hands of his——'

President Dayles didn't hear the rest. His mind stopped on the words 'two hands.'

He stood up and shook hands with the delighted old man. 'Now listen, my friend,' said President Dayles, 'from this moment your name goes on a special file, and any time you want a favor from the White House, write to my secretary, and if it can be done it will be done. Meanwhile, you will, I hope, continue to be silent about this interview as a duty to your country.'

'You can count on me,' said the man with the quiet positivity of sublime and unquestioning patriotism. 'An' you can forget about special favors.'

'The offer remains open,' said Dayles heartily, 'with my very best wishes.'

Afterward Kay said, 'He sounded as if he meant it—a rare type these days. Democracy is tottering.'

'You look as if you have proof,' he said. 'What's happened?'

Silently she handed him a message. He read it aloud. 'The Supreme Court upheld the sentence of death on the election rioters.' He whistled softly, then said, 'They really made a fight of it but here they are a year later at the end of the trail.' He gazed down at her thoughtfully. 'What grounds did the Court give for its verdict?'

'They didn't give reasons.'

He was silent. He also considered it a sign of the times that the original trial judgment had not been reversed.

Kay interrupted his thought. 'Now don't you interfere in

this!' she said in a severe tone

The great man said nothing.

Three days before the date set for their execution in December 1977, all of the seventeen men condemned for the parade killings staged a mass escape from the death house.

There were riots in a dozen cities, and mass delegations of women demanded punishment for the prison guards responsible and immediate recapture and execution of the escaped men.

'I thought those women were peace lovers,' said Jefferson Dayles. But he said it in private to Kay. Publicly he promised all possible action would be taken.

On the second day following this speech a letter arrived at the Special File, a letter that read:

> *Cell 676, Kaggat Prison*
> *January 27, 1978*

Dear Mr. President:

I have learned that my husband was one of the seventeen condemned men, and I know where he and they are. Speed is essential if his life is to be saved. Please hurry.

ANRELLA PENDRAKE

Kay waited with flashing eyes until he had read the message, then she handed him a report from the FBI, which read:

'There was a great deal of confusion at the time of the arrest of these men. None was fingerprinted until the day after the sentencing. Then all the original photos and fingerprints were lost. This was not discovered until the men were transferred to a maximum security prison, and it is significant that en route to this prison the bus carrying them went into a ditch. There was a claim made by several of the prisoners that one man disappeared at this time and that another man was substituted for him. The authorities at the new prison were not inclined to accept this wild tale, since none of the seventeen reported himself as having been victimized. To prevent such talk, they separated the men——'

Kay interrupted him at that point. 'Pendrake must have been the one substituted. It's impossible that he participated in that riot. We'd have to postulate a coincidence of such an order——'

'But how did they find him when we couldn't?' interjected President Dayles.

Kay was silent. Finally: 'We'd better go and have a talk with that woman,' she said.

The cell did not look as comfortable as he had originally ordered it should be. Jefferson Dayles made a mental note to deliver a sharp reprimand on the matter, then turned his attention to the pale creature that was Anrella Pendrake.

It was his first face-to-face contact. And in spite of her bleached appearance, he felt impressed. There was something about her eyes—a dignity and power, a maturity—that was disturbing. After that first impression, the dullness of her voice surprised him. She sounded more beaten than she looked.

Anrella Pendrake said: 'No, I *want* to tell you. Jim is in hiding on the great California desert. The ranch is located about forty miles north of the village of Mountainside——' She broke off. 'Please don't ask me under what circumstances he did what he did. The important thing is to make sure when you find his hideout that he is not killed.' She smiled wanly. 'Our original belief was that, as a group, we could through him dominate world affairs. I'm afraid we overestimated our capabilities.'

Kay said, 'Mrs. Pendrake, we absolutely must have an explanation of how it was possible for you to find your husband, when, with all the resources of the U.S. intelligence, we were unable to do so.'

The woman in the cell smiled wanly for the first time in the interview. 'When we first got hold of Jim,' she said, 'we embedded a tiny transistor device in the muscles of his shoulder. It gives off a signal that we can detect. Does that answer your question?'

President Dayles answered, 'It certainly does. You could have located him at any time?'

'Yes,' Anrella answered.

With that, they left her.

On the northbound plane, Kay said, 'I see no reason why either Mrs. Pendrake or any of the others should be released. Now that she has so foolishly revealed her ace in the hole, Pendrake's identity as one of the parade killers, we owe her nothing.'

There was an interruption: 'A radiogram message, Mr. President, from Kaggat Prison.'

Jefferson Dayles read the long message with pursed lips, then handed it without a word to Kay.

'Escaped!' Kay cried. 'The whole gang!' She sat very still. 'Why, the white-faced little actress, standing there pretending to be depressed to the point of nothing-else-matters-but-that-he-be-saved. But why did she tell us? Why?'

She stopped, reread the message, and whispered finally, 'Did you see this? Ninety planes fitted with that special engine participated in the rescue! What an organization they must have. It means the escape could have been managed at any time. And yet they waited until now. Sir, this is very serious.'

Jefferson Dayles felt curiously remote from his assistant's near panic. His mood was exhilaration, and there was in him an intense and gathering will to victory. The situation was indeed serious; here, in fact, was a crisis. Nevertheless, his voice was calm as he said, 'Kay, we'll use five divisions, two of them armored, and as many planes as we need—not ninety, but nine hundred. We'll surround the desert. We'll check all traffic on the land or in the air, moving out of it. Use radar detectors at night, searchlights, night fighters. We'll use the unlimited power of the armed force of the United States. Capture Pendrake!'

He was, he realized, fighting for his life.

Twenty-three

The whining winds of winter blew steadily in January. On the fifteenth a blizzard buried nearly all New York State and Pennsylvania. People awakened on the morning of the sixteenth to a world that was again white and pure and peaceful.

That same day, far to the south, Hoskins and Cree Lipton, after investigating clues that had led them to South America, took off from the bulge of Brazil and headed for Germany via Dakar, Algiers, and Vichy.

American headquarters on Unter den Linden in Berlin was their destination, and in the great, thick-carpeted Red Room on the second floor a top American general quickly led them to a guarded room.

'This,' he indicated with his hand, 'is what we call our murder map. In view of the watch we've been keeping for you the past few weeks, the map has become an amazingly interesting document.'

The map was thirty feet long and covered with colored pins—hardly a 'document,' Hoskins thought wryly. But he said nothing, simply watched and listened with an anxious will to hear the end result.

'A month ago to the day,' the general said, 'we sent out trucks all over what was formerly occupied Europe with the posters asking for information about the engine, the poster having been worded according to your cabled instructions.'

He pulled out a package of cigarettes, offered them to the two men; Hoskins declined with a tiny inclination of his head and waited impatiently while the others lighted up. The officer went on, 'Now, before I tell you the extent and limitations of our success, I think it is necessary to describe briefly the situation that exists in Germany today. As you know, Hitler's method was to put a party man into every conceivable controlling position in every community. In West Germany we long ago deposed all these petty führers, replacing them with the staunchest prewar democrats we could find. In East Germany the Soviets tried to use many of Hitler's people, rightly seeing that Communist and Nazi terrorists were actually brothers under the skin. What they did not grasp was that the better-educated Germans would never in their hearts accept the average Slav as an equal—not yet, not this generation—pound in Lenin's doctrine on nationalities as they might.

'Not till we told the Soviets your findings did the truth penetrate—that a secret, entirely pro-German terrorist group had formed right under their noses in East Germany. That's when they let our men in, and so here is what we've found : Right now, Germans are committing about a thousand murders a week in East Germany itself, about eight hundred more in the rest of Europe.'

'How does this affect the finding of information about the engine and about the seven missing scientists whose bodies and whose families we couldn't find in the U.S.A.?' asked the heavy-jawed Lipton.

'We made a murder graph of every district in Europe,' was the reply, 'and as the appeal for information spread, we watched day by day for any upswing in murders, the assumption being that great precautions would be taken by the Nazis in districts where information existed.'

He faced the two men, a grim smile on his face.

'I report accordingly, with mixed feelings, that the number of murders in two widely separated territories, one in Hohenstein in Saxony, the other in the town of Latsky, Bulgaria, increased out of all normal proportion.'

'Bulgaria !' It was Lipton, his tone puzzled.

Hoskins said quickly, 'After all, our closest watch has always been on Germany proper. They must have found it easier to set up interplanetary bases among certain sympathetic people; of these, the Bulgarians were undoubtedly the most unwilling victims of communism.'

The general looked at him from shrewd brown eyes. 'Exactly. We've made a very cautious survey of these two districts. On the third day of our search we found a luxuriously furnished mine shaft at Hohenstein that evidently had been hastily abandoned.

'Questioning among townsmen,' the officer went on, 'elicited the information that a strange Zeppelin-like machine had been seen at night in the vicinity of the abandoned shaft.'

'Good heavens!'

Hoskins was scarcely aware that he had uttered the exclamation. He realized after a blank moment that he had been listening to the general with a vague impatience, an anxiety to have an end of words and to get actively on with the search. And now——

It was all done. The search was over, or almost over. All preliminaries were successfully concluded.

'Sir,' he said warmly, 'you are a remarkable man.'

'Let me finish.' The officer smiled broadly. 'I'm not through yet.'

He went on in a precise tone. 'We have received altogether three—out of thousands—letters that are unmistakably genuine and relevant. The third, and most important, from a Frau Kreigmeier, wife of the man who has been the Bulgarian Nazi party leader in Latsky for three years, arrived last night when I had already received word that you were on your way here.

'Gentlemen'—his voice was quiet but confident—'by the end of the week you will have all the information that is still available on this continent.

'Naturally,' he finished, and his careful phrasing of his promise had already brought the first shock to Hoskins, 'the Nazis will have made every effort to insure that nothing vital is available. Nevertheless——'

By noon of February 4 they had the bodies of the Lambton Land Settlement Project people. Seven older men, nine women, two girls, and twelve youths lay side by side on the cold ground. Silently they were loaded onto hearses and started on the journey to the coast, from where they would be shipped to America for more fitting burial.

After the hearses had disappeared down the road, Hoskins stood with the others in the little clump of bushes where they had been led by the plump husband of Frau Kreigmeier. A cold north wind was blowing, and the men in the armored cars that had escorted them were beating their hands together for warmth.

In spite of the cold, Hoskins noted ferociously, Herr Kreigmeier was sweating profusely. 'If ever a man deserved hanging——' he thought.

But they had promised: the posters had promised—

money, safe removal, and unlimited police protection.

The general came up. 'The shovel men will finish up here,' he said. 'Let's go. I crave the warmth of a hotel room. You can mull over the successes and'—he looked quickly at Hoskins—'the failures.'

There wasn't much to examine. Silently Hoskins sat in his chair before a roaring grate fire and reread the translation of the single note they had resurrected :

'Movement of anything requires a reverse movement, a cancellation, a balancing. A body moving between two points in space uses energy, which is another word for reverse movement.

'The science of reverse movement involved in its greatest functions a relationship between the microcosmos and the macrocosmos, between the infinitely small and the infinitely large. When a balance is established between two forces of the macrocosmos, one loses what the other gains.

'Engines puff noisily; organic creatures laboriously perform their duties. Life seems infinitely hard.

'However, when a reverse movement is created in the microcosmos for a movement occurring in the macrocosmos, then the ultimate in energy relations is obtained. There is also a complete balancing result; the law that movement is equal to reverse movement holds as rigidly as before——'

'I'd hate,' said Hoskins wearily, 'to ask any patent office to grant a patent on that. I'm afraid we've reached the end of the engine trail, and that means my hope for quick action that would rescue Pendrake and his wife is gone. The rest of this stuff'—he flicked the typewritten sheet—'consists of notes on engineering problems of installation. There's a big gap somewhere, and I guess it's the hole in the empty sack we're holding.'

He looked up. 'Anything new from Hohenstein, the other murder center ?'

'Nothing,' said Cree Lipton. 'It was obviously only one of their ports of call for spaceships, hastily evacuated during our search. They've got their main equipment, all their secrets, on Mars or Venus——'

Hoskins cut in : 'The moon! Make no mistake about it.

Mars or Venus would be too far away even at their closest. And besides, they wouldn't dare let their young men and women see the kind of planet that Venus must be if you can believe the report of what the Lambton Land Settlement Project promised its settlers. It's blood and iron the German leaders have in mind—rescue of East Germany and reunion of their country. Until that is accomplished, the leaders will keep the lower ranks on a diet of hard work, hard environment and hope. They haven't had time to get really good bases established anywhere. So I think you and I had better get back to America. We have things to do.'

It was three days later.

President Dayles, on his way to Mountainside, California, sat in the helicar with Cree Lipton and listened to the report on the East German resurgence and to the urgent request for men and money to go to the moon. He nodded his complete agreement.

'Yes, yes,' he said, 'do that, also. We've got the satellites up. We can step gingerly over to the moon at fabulous expense—but I can justify diverting War Department funds to the job if it means stopping the last remnant of the Hitler gang. Get as many rockets out of mothballs as you need. I think we manufactured ten thousand before we arrived at our agreement with the Soviets that it was indeed a great universe up there but that it had no practical value till we could go up without bankrupting our countries. Rockets aren't cheap enough.'

He went on ruefully, 'Those who did find a better way didn't trust us as bullies to use their discovery properly. And then—as you and they have discovered—they collided with the madness of suppressed nationalism. We're a pretty crazy world, Mr. Lipton.'

Kay, who had been listening in silence, now spoke. 'Mr. Lipton, did you say that one of the purposes of your associate, Mr. Hoskins, is to rescue Jim Pendrake and his wife from the Nazis on the moon?'

'Yes.' The big man seemed surprised.

There was a pause. The President and his secretary exchanged swift glances. 'Fill us in on that,' said President Dayles finally.

Lipton did so and concluded, 'When we investigated Mrs. Pendrake's disappearance, it developed that a plane had landed on the estate and that she went off in that. The note she left, the manner of her departure, the description of how the plane rose into the air indicated that it was a kidnaping—and by someone who possessed this very special type of aircraft.'

The Chief Executive turned to Kay. 'Can you give me any reason why the information about the disappearance of Mrs. Pendrake was never brought to my attention?'

The woman shrugged. 'Millions of data come to the Pentagon. Only a small bit of it is ever sent to the White House.'

President Dayles pursed his lips. 'Well, that presumably takes Mrs. Pendrake to the moon. But why assume that Mr. Pendrake also made the journey?'

Lipton explained about the message from Mrs. Pendrake to the effect that her husband had gone to the Lambton Towers. He finished, 'Since—as we have discovered—that was taken over by the East German conspiratorial group, we may assume that Pendrake was captured or killed. If captured, then he might well have been taken off the planet. Mr. Hoskins is personally interested in the welfare of the Pendrakes. The two men fought in the same air unit in Asia'.

President Dayles, who was also interested in the welfare of James Pendrake, merely nodded.

The papers which authorized the armed forces to prepare secretly for an invasion of the moon were signed in a tiny office in the Mountainside Inn by a disguised Chief Executive.

After Lipton had left, Kay said, 'A lot of questions remain unanswered. If Pendrake was taken to the moon, how did he escape the Germans? How did he get back here?'

Pendrake awakened. It wasn't anything to think about. Where there had been blankness was suddenly light. He lay very still. He had no consciousness that he had a name or that there was anything unusual about the situation. *He* was here—the entity that was himself—lying down. Even the posture seemed normal, the very essence of life as it was lived. He was lying down, and aware of himself.

For a long time that was all there was. He had no purpose other than being where he was, no memory of anything else, not the faintest conception of movement. He lay, and he stared up at a ceiling that was light blue in color. It was not the brightest region in his universe, and so, after a while, his gaze was drawn to the window through which light blazed dazzlingly.

Like a child absorbed by shiningness, he brought up his arm and reached toward the window. The intervening emptiness rebuffed him. Instantly that didn't matter, because he became interested in his groping arm. He did realize that the arm was part of himself. The moment he ceased his instinctive reaching, the muscles that supported the arm in the air began to relax. The arm collapsed onto the bed. And because his gaze had followed its clumsy fall, for the first time he grew aware of the bed. He was still examining it, half sitting up, the better to look at it, when the sound of footsteps intruded upon his attention.

The sound came nearer, but he did not wonder about it. It was there in his ears, as normal as everything else. The difference was, he was suddenly mentally divided into two sections. One part remained in the bed. The other stared out at the world through the eyes of a man who was coming through an adjoining room toward the door of the bedroom.

He knew the other entity was a man and that the room door and act of walking were what they were because, to the second part of his mind, those facts were casual realities of life. The second mind was aware of other things too; and so rapid, so completely absorbent was his own brain, that as the door opened he swung his legs off the bed and said :

'Bring my clothes, will you, Peters?'

Peters' brain took the impact of the demand with complete acquiescence. He went out, and there was a satisfying mind picture of him fumbling in a clothes closet. He came back and paused just inside the door, blinking with new thought. He was a little man in shirt sleeves, carrying a lot of clothing. He peered over them and said owlishly, 'Lordy, Bill, you can't get up yet. You were still unconscious half an hour ago when we caught that dame in here.' He added solicitously, 'I'll call the doc and bring you some hot soup. After the way you got us out of the death house, we're taking no chances of anything going wrong with you. Lie back, will you?'

Pendrake, watching the other lay the clothes on a chair, hesitated. The argument seemed reasonable, yet somehow not quite applicable to him. After a moment he still hadn't put a mental finger on the flaw. His hesitation ended. He drew his legs back under the quilt and said, 'Maybe you've got something there. But the way that woman was captured right in this room started me worrying about our hideout here.'

He stopped with a frown. Flashing insight came that he hadn't been worried until Peters appeared on the scene and that in fact his mental state at the beginning had been— what? The memory galvanized his thought. His mind twisted back to the moment of his regaining consciousness. It was amazingly hard to picture himself as he had been at that first instant, blank-brained, without memory. And then instantly absorbing the entire mind of Peters, with all Peters' fears and emotional immaturities. What was utterly astounding was that his memory took in Peters' mind and Peters' knowledge. But nothing else. Nothing of himself.

He stared at the man. That profound but swift examination took in all Peters' memory and went back through the simple career of a chunky boy who wanted to be a mechanic. No particular reason existed why Peters should have joined the mob that attacked the parade of women. And the actual mob scene was blurred, the trial that followed a nightmare of twisting through forms dominated by fears so terrible that not a single image came clear. The fear had faded into excited hope during the escape, and so there was a reasonably detailed remembrance of exactly how the prison break had been worked three days before the date set for the mass gassing.

'Did I really do all that?' Pendrake thought incredulously.

After a moment the fact was still there, a rigid part of Peters' memory of the event. He had taken apart the radio in his cell and, with the addition of parts from radios handed to him from other cells, had manufactured a very pale white light that ate through concrete and steel as if they were insubstantial matter. A guard confronting them had screamed as his gun dissolved in his hands, his clothes disintegrated from his body. The scream must have been pure hysteria, because that pale, intense fire had not harmed him.

The very nature of the weapon, and the mode of exit it provided, prevented the reinforcements brought by the scream from being effective. The police didn't think of solid walls being breached. The cars were at the arranged rendezvous, and the planes, each with its pilot, were concealed beside the grass field across which they took off.

All this was in Peters' memory, as well as the fact that the man known as Bill Smith had been hit by a machine-gun bullet as the cars raced away from the prison—the only casualty but one who was carefully looked after. For days now he had lain unconscious.

Pendrake pondered about it while Peters went for the soup. He decided finally that he was different. It needed only the simplest reflection to realize that reading thoughts, actually absorbing another's mind, was unheard of in Peters' lexicon of life. He was slowly sipping his soup when Doc McLarg came in. Seen face to face, and not merely as a memory image of Peter's transferred mind, the doctor was a spare-built man about thirty-five and possessed of shrewd brown eyes. The history behind that physical exterior was more complicated than that of Peters, but the relevant facts were simple. A public health officer, McLarg had been forced to resign because of careless work and he was replaced by a woman doctor. On Christmas Eve, in an advanced state of poverty and drunkenness, he had joined lustily in the attack on the parading women.

His examination was that of a nonplused man. 'It's beyond me,' he confessed finally. 'Three days ago I cut a machine-gun bullet out of your chest, and for twenty-four hours there hasn't been either an entrance or an exit wound. If I didn't know it was impossible, I'd guess you were perfectly well.'

There seemed nothing to say to that. McLarg's mind had slipped so gently into him, its knowledge so easily and naturally integrated with that derived from Peters, that even now it was hard to grasp that the information hadn't been there all the time.

He thought about the woman later, frowningly. She had been in his room, bending over him. She had just walked in, she had said. Walked in unseen—into a den of alert, hunted outlaws!

It seemed ridiculous. Uncertain what to do with her, the men had finally locked her in one of the spare rooms of the hacienda. It was odd that, though the house blurred and wavered with thoughts as men went tensely to and fro, hers was not among them. Not once did he catch even a tendril of mind stuff that might belong to a woman. Surely a woman's thoughts would be unmistakable.

Sleep found Pendrake still puzzling over the whole problem of her.

Twenty-five

He awakened with a start in pitch-darkness, conscious that there was someone in the room.

'Quiet!' the woman's voice whispered in his ear. 'This is a gun.'

The paralyzing thing was that he still couldn't catch a glimmer of her thought. His mind leaped to his earlier speculation on the subject and then to a simple conclusion: *He couldn't read the minds of women!*

He said blankly, 'What do you want?'

In the darkness he felt the metal press against his head, and his thought suffered a dreadful pause. The woman spoke again. 'Take your clothes—never mind dressing—and walk slowly to the door of your clothes closet. There is an open panel inside with steps leading down. Go down them!'

In a sweat of mental anguish he fumbled for his clothes. He was thinking: How could she have escaped from her room? 'I wish,' he whispered hoarsely, 'the others had killed you instead of just arguing about it, you——'

He stopped, because the gun was pressing against the back of his pajama coat, urging him along.

'Quiet!' came the peremptory whisper. 'The truth is, Jim, you're to be given a few facts about yourself before the authorities close in, as they will do very shortly. Now, please hurry.'

'What did you call me?'

'Move!'

He walked slowly, but his mind was tightening around the tremendous reality that she knew him. This woman they had captured, this—what had she said her name was? —Anrella Pendrake *knew* his real identity.

He had had a vague plan of whirling on her in the darkness and grabbing her gun. But that was shattered by her words.

He had to squeeze through the panel, it was so narrow. The staircase was a winding affair that led steeply downward. After the first full turn, a series of tiny costobulbs began. Their misty rays made the passageway seem more alive, more real. For the first time, the fact of them made an impact on his brain. Here was an old ranch house to which seventeen condemned murderers had fled turning out to be honey-combed with secret panels. It couldn't possibly be an accident.

One swift grab at her legs, he decided.

'Jim!' Her voice was a sigh from behind him. 'I swear that this will not add one iota to the danger you are all in. When you consider that it was our organization that placed those cars and planes at your disposal when you escaped from the prison, you——'

'What?' He stopped, protested. 'Listen, those cars and planes were given us by the friend of——'

'An individual giving four cars and two planes? Don't be silly.'

'But——'

He broke off, fascinated by her logic; then, 'You keep calling me Jim. Jim what?'

'Jim Pendrake.'

'But your name is Anrella Pendrake.'

'That's right. You're my husband. Now, move down those steps.'

'If you're my wife,' Pendrake flashed, 'you'll prove it by giving me the gun and trusting me. Give it to me.'

The weapon was thrust so quickly past his shoulder that he blinked at it, then reached for it gingerly, half expecting it to be withdrawn. It wasn't. His fingers closed over it; hers released it. He stood with the gun, nonplused by the easy victory, feeling stripped of all possibilities of violence.

'Please go down,' her voice came.

'But who is Jim Pendrake?'

'You will know in a few minutes. Now, please.'

He went. Down, down, down. Twice they passed solid steel plates that pressed out to every wall of the staircase, like floors of protective battleship deck metal. The thickness of them made Pendrake stare. Eight inches. *Each!*

Here was a fortress.

The end came suddenly. A narrow corridor, a door, and then a blaze of lights, a great room filled with machines. There were doors leading to other rooms, tantalizing glimpses of gleaming staircases that went down—tantalizing because they suggested other great tiers of rooms below. The weight began to lift from his mind; the weight of conviction that he and Peters and the others had no chance of escape. Here, in this subterranean world, was safety!

He felt the surge of new life, of hope. It was a sudden alertness, a glow suffusing his whole being. His gaze flashed the rounds of the machine room, questioningly. His mind strained to locate signs of human occupancy. He had time to notice keenly that even the thoughts of Peters and the others did not penetrate into these metallically sealed depths.

A door opened in the wall to his right. Three men emerged. The physical act of the emergence scarcely mattered. At the very instant of the door opening, their thoughts darted out to him.

It was a small flood of pictures and ideas about himself, his past, his life.

Through that turmoil of impression, he heard one of the men whisper to the woman: 'Any trouble?'

'None,' she replied. 'All the elaborate precautions were unnecessary. Their search was cursory. They did talk half-heartedly about killing me, but I could have prevented that at any time. Not once did anyone suggest examining the buttons of my clothes for lethal gases. After all, they're fundamentally not criminals.... But, sssshh now, let him get what's in your minds without interruption.'

The picture that came was restricted as to time. It began with Nypers hinting to him that something was wrong. And it ended here in this fortress with a deadly plane. Their knowledge of his life was quite limited.

Pendrake broke the silence in a strained, astounded voice: 'Am I to understand that Peters, McLarg, and I, with Kelgar, Rainey, and the others, are going to be kept up there on the surface while the United States armed forces try to capture us? And you're going to stand by and watch us try to figure a way out but do nothing to help us?'

He saw that his—wife—was nodding with a faint smile.

The amusement faded. Her eyes became bright and oddly sympathetic. 'You're in the spotlight, Jim. You've got to do even better than when you escaped from the jail. You've got to lift yourself almost literally by your mental bootstraps and temporarily become a superman. You see—you're in the final phase of your final change. Whatever you raise yourself to now will be permanent. No more changes.'

Her eyes grew suddenly moist. She reached forward impulsively and caught his arm. 'Jim, don't you see? If we weakened now, we'd be failing you and all those other people out there in that poor, confused world. ... Jim, we've resolved that none of us will survive if you fail. So our fate is bound up with yours. Listen, here below ground is a marvelous machine-shop. In a few minutes the greatest male scientists in our organization will be brought in one by one—and you can take the massive knowledge in their minds and make it your own. I'm sorry you can't read the minds of women, because we have some wonderful women scientists.'

She led him to a chair, sat down opposite him, and said :

'Jim, we toti-potents—you and I and a few others—are an accident which all started with the finding of a remarkable engine. Each of us can give blood every few months to people of our blood type, and so they recover their youthfulness also. But none has ever become toti-potent as a result of such a transfusion. This ties them to us with inhumanly strong bonds, because they must presently have some of our blood again or they start to age once more.

'When you consider that every toti-potent has at least twice the average brain capacity, you can see that we represent the beginning of a breakthrough into something new and greater for the human race. For example, we solved the secret of the Lambton engine. No one else has, or can. The Germans captured more than eighty per cent of our engines, and that was quite a haul, but that's all they've got. Yet even our normal brain capacity is only a fraction of what is possible. We know that, because some of us attained as much as twenty times the average human during those gray, unremembered months that make up a toti-potent period.

'Listen, here is my story, my little bit of evidence. I was born in 1896, became a nurse in World War I, and had my right arm torn off by a high explosive shell. It must have been the mud that saved me from bleeding to death. For days I lay untended, and note this well : There is no record of anyone becoming toti-potent who has not a background of pressure on them. That's our only clue. A body given prompt medical attention cannot become toti-potent. Nothing happened at the time of course, but later when I worked on a Lambton research program I was exposed to the engine, and my arm grew back and my youth was restored.'

'Where did the Lambton engine come from?' Pendrake asked.

'That,' the woman confessed, 'is the mystery. Mr. Lambton claimed that his grandfather was found dead in it some time in the 1870's. He had tried to land it on the family farm but the machine evidently struck the ground too hard. At the last minute he must have realized what was going to happen, for he opened the door and tried to leap out. The story is that he was found dead half in, half out of the door. When they pulled the broken body free, the door of the craft shut automatically, and no one could get into it again. It wasn't heavy so they dragged it into the rear of one of the big barns, and it lay there for three quarters of a century, according to Mr. Lambton. When they tore down the old building, they found it; he remembered the story and had the craft transported to the foundation. That is when Dr. Grayson discovered what it was.'

She continued after a pause, 'During the second phase of my toti-potent period, I invented a little metal water-repellent plate. When one of these was fastened to the bottom of each of my shoes I was able to walk on water. We still can't be sure how they work. We assume that I must have been in great danger from death by drowning, but we don't know even that. We can't duplicate them, although they appear to be constructed from the ordinary materials one might find aboard a ship. That is the real glory of it. This vast earth of ours, with its multitude of inventions, apparently needs only a sharper mind to grasp at the facts that lie under our eyes among the everyday things of life. Training and education are a substitute for this, but not a very good one.

'Jim, you know your task. Above ground you will find an assortment of machines. Engines, tools, electronic and electrical instruments, something of almost everything. Those dozen outbuildings are full of what seems to be junk, but it isn't. Look over everything, and let your mind try to create new combinations of those old forms. The moment you have something, communicate with the men down here. They'll build anything you want in a few hours.

'Jim, our own experience in idealistic work has been sad. Something more is needed. We want to make one more try before we decide either to leave man alone or continue trying to force a faster development of civilization. Do you understand?'

As Pendrake was led to his bedroom, it seemed to him that their purpose couldn't have been expressed more clearly.

He kept awakening in a sweat of fear. Twice, lying in a half doze, he told himself that he had dreamed his visit into the fortress under the ranch house. But each time a grimmer realization was there to chide his mind for its illusions. The day before, with the danger seemingly remote, he had dallied with the hope that they might actually be safe in their desert hideout. Now he knew better. An army of tanks and planes would attack——

His thoughts followed an uneven course through the long night. Once a wonder came: This twenty-times-average capacity of the human brain—it couldn't be IQ. Only an electronic thinking machine could have an IQ of 2000. There were other factors in the brain that might be affected. How was it, for instance, that a person with an IQ of 100 frequently had twice the personality and leadership qualities of some freak with an IQ of 160? No, the 20-brain wouldn't be IQ. It would be—he couldn't imagine.

He must have slept on the thought. When he awoke, it was still dark, and there was decision in him. He would try. He felt no different, no exceptional ability to create, but he would try.

As dawn broke, Jefferson Dayles rose and stared through the eye-holes of his perfect flesh mask, out through the window of Mountainside Inn. It was the waiting, he thought. All that he could do had been done. The orders, the intricate planning, the details of insuring that no escape avenues remained open—all that, he had attended to personally. And now others must do the work while he paced helplessly to and fro in the confined space of this small room—waiting.

The door behind him opened, but he did not turn.

The shadows lay heavy on the desert, but the mountains to the right were visible against the lightening sky. And to the left among the scatter of trees beyond the village, he could see the white tents of the awakening army.

Kay said from behind him, 'I've brought your breakfast.'

He had forgotten that someone had come in. He jumped from the impact of the voice. And then smiled grimly at himself. He turned and said, 'Breakfast?'

He drank his orange juice and ate the kidney on toast in silence. When he had finished, Kay spoke again. 'I'm pretty certain no one suspects your presence.' She added after a moment, 'We'll start in about an hour. It will require at least three hours to cover the forty miles over the sand. Some of our scouts penetrated to within a few hundred yards of the house during the night without being challenged. However, they obeyed orders and made no attempt to invade the yard.' She finished, 'I'm beginning to think our precautions have been ridiculous, but I agree that it's better to be sure than sorry. There is no longer any doubt. We must have this man before we can even think of a third term.'

No answer. Four hours, Jefferson Dayles was thinking, four hours before he would know his fate.

Twenty-six

At the ranch, the chill of the desert night faded into a cold dawn which slowly warmed that gray land. The men were up early. They ate breakfast almost in silence, offered no objections to Pendrake's statement about the prisoner hereafter being in his charge, and finally dispersed. Some went out to relieve the night watchers on the peaks that topped the gashed hills and uneven sand plains. Only one or two actually seemed busy.

The atmosphere was tense, nervous, expectant. As they closed the door of the third outhouse, Anrella said frowning, 'I certainly expected the men to object when you said that I would accompany you wherever you went today. It must have puzzled them.'

Pendrake was silent. The mantle of leadership that had been yielded to him puzzled him also. Several times he had caught the beginning of opposition in the minds of the men, only to watch it fade away without being given expression. He grew aware that Anrella was speaking again, uneasily. 'I wish I hadn't advised you to go back to sleep. We wanted you to be fresh for your task. But we also wanted to time everything so that you would have at least half a day.'

Curiously, just like that, her words irritated him. He said sharply, 'My means to success are too limited. And I have a conviction I'm approaching this whole subject from the wrong angle It's the mechanical slant that's not right. I could see several possibilities, for instance, in the electrical equipment in that last outhouse. The use of the 999-plus vacuum offers several opportunities when conjuncted with electrical coils, but——'

He stared at her darkly. 'There's one fatal flaw in them all. They kill. They burn and destroy. Frankly, I'll be hanged before I murder a bunch of poor soldiers doing their duty. And I might as well tell you right now I'm getting fed up.' He waved his arm impatiently. 'This whole business is too silly for words. I'm beginning to wonder if I'm in my right mind.' He scowled at her angrily. 'Let me ask you a question. Is it possible for you to have a spaceship here in a short time to pick us all up and so save the lives of everyone above ground here?'

Anrella's gaze was quiet, her manner tranquil. 'It's even simpler than that. We could take you below ground. But the spaceship is available too. There's one about twenty miles above us, a large model of what you used to think was an electric plane. I could call it down right now. But I won't. This is the critical moment in a plan we have been maturing ever since we first found you.'

Pendrake snapped, 'I don't believe your threat about killing yourselves. That's merely another pressure trick.'

Anrella said softly, 'You're tired, Jim, and under great physical strain. I swear on my word of honor that what I have told you is the truth.'

'What's ordinary honor to a superwoman?'

She was calm. 'If you think about the implications of your refusal to kill the people who are coming to attack us, you will realize that what makes everything we do so right is that our intentions are honorable, Jim, I'm over eighty years old. Physically, of course, I don't feel it, but mentally I do. And so do the others. Seventeen of them are older than I am, twelve about the same age. It's strange that so few totipotent potentials came out of the last war; perhaps the medical services were better, but never mind that. All of us have seen a lot, thought a lot. And we feel sincerely that we can only be a hindrance to the human race unless we can somehow influence them along the paths of progress. To that end, we must have stronger, abler leadership than anything we have so far managed ourselves. We——'

There was a tiny *ting* from her jewel wrist radio. She lifted it, so that he could hear too. A small but clear voice said, 'A column of armored cars and several tanks are streaming along the road that leads to Arroyo Pass ten miles south of Mountainside. A number of planes have been passing over here since dawn. If you haven't seen them, it must mean they're keeping out of sight of the ranch. That's all.'

The minute *ting* repeated. And there was silence.

Anrella broke it in a strained voice. She said, 'I think, Jim, we had better get back to realities. I'm beginning to believe it's important that we have a preliminary weapon that will hold off land armies and give you time to develop a major invention. We won't have to worry about aerial bombing, I'm sure, because the last thing Jefferson Dayles desires is your destruction.' She hesitated. 'What about that disintegrating ray which affects only inorganic matter?' Her blue eyes gave him a quick, questioning glance. 'We're willing to supply the wire to the nearest electric plug, just as we did in the jail. Or even a mobile power plant.' Once more she hesitated; then, 'It would destroy their tanks, armored cars, and would strip them to their birthday suits.' She laughed nervously. 'That would disorganize almost any army now in existence.'

Pendrake shook his head. 'I examined it just before breakfast. And it's no go. It's complete as is. I could reduce it to the size of a hand weapon and retain the same power. But an increase in bulk would add no energy. It all depends on one tube that——'

He shrugged. 'All they have to do is verify that I'm not manning it, then keep their artillery beyond its quarter-mile range and probe with high explosives. It's possible'—he smiled savagely—'that one of the men would rather die that way than in a gas chamber. But you can see it's no solution. What are you doing, Haines?'

They had come to where a well-set, unshaven young man was working on the engine of a car. The hood was up, and he was standing with one of the spark plugs in his fingers brushing its points. Actually, Pendrake's question was unnecessary. Clearly delineated in the man's mind was the intention to get the engine working and leave the ranch.

Dan Haines was a bit-part actor whose only reason for participating in the parade attack had been, as he had stated sullenly to the court, that he couldn't stand a 'world run by women' and that he had 'got excited.' And also that he was ready to take 'what was coming to him.' He had added nothing to the escape except the burden of his jittery presence. And now, in a jump of apprehension, his nerve had broken. He looked up guilty. 'Oh!' he said as he saw Anrella. Then, more casually, 'Just fixing the bus. I want us to be able to make a run for it if we have to.'

Pendrake stepped past him and stared down curiously at the exposed engine. In his mind's eye he was visualizing the whole machine, first as a unit, then each separate function

in detail. It was a lightning examination and purely mental—
engine, battery, ignition, clutch, generator—— He paused
there and went back : battery——

He said slowly, 'What would happen, Haines, if all the
power of a battery was discharged in a hundred-billionth of
a second?'

'Huh !' said Haines blankly. 'That couldn't happen.'

'It would,' said Pendrake, 'if the lead plate is electrically
prehardened and if you use a pentagrid shielding tube, the
type of tube that is used to control unwanted power. It——'

He stopped. Suddenly the details stood sharp and clear in
his mind. He made a mental calculation and then, looking
up, saw Anrella's shining eyes on him.

After a moment her gaze darkened. She said, startled. 'I
see what you're getting at. But wouldn't the temperature be
too great? The figures I get are unbelievable.'

'We can use a miniature battery,' Pendrake said quickly.
'After all, it's merely the percussion cap. The reason the
temperature would be so high is that in the interior of a sun
there is no control tube, and so the right environment
occurs only here and there through space, and we have a
Nova-O sun.

'With a normal-sized battery the temperature would be
too high. But I think we could strip off the four most
dangerous zeros by using a small, short-lived dry cell, and so
be safe. It would, of course, chain-react, but the result
would be a point of heat, not an explosion. And it would
last for several hours.' He paused, frowning, then said,
'Don't leave, Haines. Stay right here on the ranch.'

'All right.'

Pendrake walked off thoughtfully, and then once more he
stopped. 'That,' he thought, 'was pretty quick agreement.
How come?'

Wide-eyed, he whirled and stared at Haines. The man had
turned his back, but every mental contour of his brain was
exposed. Pendrake stood there, comparing, remembering;
and finally, satisfied, he faced Anrella and said quietly, 'Let
your people work on that at top speed. And work out, too,
some refrigeration system for the ranch house. I think the
battery should be buried about ten feet in the sand three
or four miles south of here. And I don't see why it should

take longer than three quarters of an hour. As for you and me'—he stared at her sardonically—'order the spaceship down. We're going to Mountainside.'

'We're what?' She looked at him, suddenly white. 'Jim, you know that doesn't follow logically out of this invention.'

He made no answer, simply stared at her; and after a moment she said, 'This is all wrong. I shouldn't do it. I——' She shook her head, bewildered. Then, without further protest, lifted her wrist radio.

By 8 a.m. the old-timers were gathered on the porch at Mountainside Inn. Pendrake could see them looking slant-eyed at Anrella and himself and at the dozen very obvious Secret Service women who lounged in various positions around the door. The oldsters of Mountainside were not accustomed to having strangers intrude upon their privacy, particularly hard-faced women. But a danged lot of things had been happening lately. Their minds showed a mixture of excitement and irritation. The conversation had a numbed quality.

It was about ten minutes after eight when one of them wiped the perspiration from his forehead and trotted to the thermometer beside the door. He came back. 'Ninety-eight.' he announced to his cronies. 'Derned warm for Mountainside this time of year.'

There was a brief, animated discussion on past heat records for the month. The cracked voices sagged slowly into an uncomfortable silence as the hot breeze from the desert blew stronger. Once more an old-timer ambled to the thermometer. He came back shaking his head. 'Hundred and five,' he said. 'And it's only twenty-five minutes after eight. Looks like it's gonna be a scorcher.'

Pendrake walked over to the men. 'I'm a doctor,' he said. 'Sudden changes in temperature like this are pretty hard on older men. Go up to Mountain Lake. Make a day of it, a holiday. But go!'

When he came back to Anrella, they were already streaming off the veranda. They roared past a few minutes later in two old sedans. Anrella frowned at Pendrake. 'The psychology of that was all wrong,' she said. 'Old desert rats don't usually accept the advice of younger men.'

'They're not desert rats,' said Pendrake. 'They're lungers.

And to them a doctor is God.' He smiled and added, 'Let's walk along the street a bit. I saw an old woman in a house there who ought to be advised to get into the hills.'

The old woman was easily persuaded by a doctor to go on a picnic. She loaded some canned goods into a wheezy old car and was off in a swirl of dust.

There was a meteorological station in a little white building fifty feet farther on. Pendrake opened the door and called to the perspiring man inside, 'What's the temperature now?'

The plump, bespectacled man dragged himself over to the desk. 'It's a hundred and twenty,' he moaned. 'It's a nightmare. The offices at Denver and Los Angeles are burning the wires asking me if I'm drunk. But'—he grimaced—'they'd better start redrawing their isobars and warn their populations. By tonight the storm winds will be raising the seats of their pants.'

Outside again, Anrella said wearily, 'Jim, please tell me what all this is about. If it gets any warmer, we'll float away on a river of perspiration.'

Pendrake laughed grimly. It was going to get warmer, all right. He felt a sudden awe. A pin point of heat—he pictured it out there to the burning south—flashing eighteen million billion degrees Fahrenheit, hotter than thousands of hydrogen bombs. The temperature here in Mountainside should go up to at least 135, and where the armored force was ... 145 ... 150. It wouldn't kill. But the officers would surely order the army to turn back and race for the cool hills.

It was hotter as they headed back to the inn. And there were other cars moving toward the mountain highway, a long line of them. The heat shimmered above the sand and against the gray hillsides. There was a dry, baked scent in the air, a stifling odor, actually painful to the lungs. Anrella said unhappily, 'Jim, are you sure you know what you're doing?'

'It's very simple.' Pendrake nodded brightly. 'I consider we've got the equivalent of a good, roaring forest fire here. If you've ever seen a forest fire—and several of my memories include knowledge on the subject—you'll know that they flush every type of game from cover. There is a mad rush toward cooler territories. Even the king of beasts condescends to run before such a conflagration. My guess was that we'd find a king here.' He finished smugly, 'There he is now, out in the open, when I can make sure with a minimum of danger that I'm not fooling myself.'

Pendrake nodded toward the inn door, from which a well-built man was emerging onto the veranda. The man's face was made up to look like that of a very ordinary middle-aged American, but his voice when he spoke was the commanding, resonant voice of Jefferson Dayles.

'Haven't you got those motors going yet?' he asked irritably. 'It seems strange, two cars getting out of order at the same moment.'

There were mumbled exclamations of apology and something about another car being along in a few minutes from the camp. Pendrake smiled and whispered to Anrella, 'I see the pilot of your spaceship is still pouring down the interfering rays. O.K. Go ahead and issue the invitation.'

'But he won't come. I'm sure he won't.'

'If he doesn't come, it will mean I've been kidding myself, and we'll head straight back to the ranch.'

'Kidding yourself about what? Jim, this is life or death for us.'

Pendrake looked at her. 'What's this?' he mocked. 'You don't like pressure? Maybe it'll double your IQ.'

Anrella stared at him; finally she said slowly, 'There must be some quality in this toti-potent phase you're in that the rest of us are not aware of.' She hesitated. 'Jim, in view of your mysterious behavior, I dare not delay with what I'm going to say now, although for personal reasons I should prefer to.'

Pendrake hesitated in turn, then rejected the idea of explaining his actions to her. Not yet. He might still need to force her in this crisis. Haines' instant acceptance of his command to stay at the ranch—and not run off as was his plan—had provided the clue. The rest—memory of how every command or determination he had expressed had been immediately acquiesced in—was confirmatory evidence. First Peters bringing his clothes and only afterward questioning the act, later Anrella handing over the gun and ordering the spaceship down, and the old men and old woman going into the mountains, proved both men and women were subject to his power.

It had nothing to do with the conscious mind. Not once had anyone been aware. It went deeper. It affected some great basic nerve structure in the brain. It must seem, to the obedient ones, that they were using their own logic. An important angle, that last. Later he would tell Anrella. Now——

Anrella was speaking again. 'I sense that you have some special ability that isn't actually good for you or for anyone, and so, before it becomes permanent'—earnestly—'Jim, *what* do you remember?'

Pendrake parted his lips to give a short summation of the vastness of his memory. And realized that it wasn't his memory at all. There were memories of half a hundred other people including, now, the total experiences of the President of the United States.

Presently, reluctantly, he explained this to her.

'Perceive the space around you!' she commanded.

It was Pendrake's turn to be bewildered. 'I don't understand. What shall I look for?'

'Your memory.'

He parted his lips again, intending to point out that the toti-potent transformation of the cells had cleared them of all impressions, a most effective erasure of his memories.

He did not utter the protest.

For he saw the energy field. It was a mental seeing, and what was amazing was that it actually seemed to have a faint glow to it. The glow was strongest near his body and grew fainter as it extended into the distance. Just how far it went, Pendrake was not quite able to determine, but he had an impression of many yards. He rejected the limitation after a moment. Distance did not seem to be a factor. He realized now that part of his knowledge included memory of the work of a Yale University scientist who had measured the electric field around each life body from the tiniest seeds to human beings.

That thought faded, because his whole life memory was flooding in on him : childhood, college, Air Force, the finding of the engine, the moon, Big Oaf, Eleanor—— 'Oh, God,' he thought. 'Eleanor—all these months—more than a year— she's been in the hands of the Neanderthal——' He groaned.

Then with an effort caught hold of the emotion that had flooded through him. 'Issue the invitation,' he said hoarsely.

The woman gazed at him compassionately. 'I don't know what you remembered,' she said, 'but you had better get a grip on yourself.'

'I'll be all right.' Pendrake said. He thought, 'First things first!' And was himself again.

Twenty-seven

Anrella turned from him and climbed the veranda steps.

He heard her in a slightly disguised voice utter the necessary words. As she finished, Pendrake called, 'Yes, come! Your car can follow.'

The President, Kay, and two equalized women followed Anrella down the steps. Anrella asked, 'Do you think we can take four?'

'Certainly,' said Pendrake. 'One can come in front here with us.'

Kay climbed into the front seat beside Anrella. A minute later the car was in medium gear and purring up the first grade.

Pendrake said, 'You know, dear, 'I've been thinking about the equalized women who make up the private army of President Dayles. The drug they took can be neutralized by a second dosage, the chemical structure of which varies slightly from the first. The crystalline manganese element in the drug as it now is, is tied to the compound by four bars. That's unstable. By removing two of the bars, the connection will be stiffened. This will——'

He broke off as, from the corners of his eyes, he saw the strained look on Anrella's face. From the rear seat, Jefferson Dayles said dryly, 'Are you a chemist, Mr.—— I didn't get the name.'

'Pendrake,' said Pendrake amiably. 'Jim Pendrake.' He went on, 'No, not a chemist. You can call me a sort of universal solvent. You see, I have discovered that I have a curious quality of the mind.' He paused. In the rear-view mirror he saw the guns that the two women in the back seat had drawn. Jefferson Dayles's voice came steadily:

'Go on, Mr. Pendrake.'

'Mr. President,' said Pendrake, 'what is weakening democracy?'

There was a long pause.

'No one can answer a question like that,' said Jefferson Dayles finally, testily. 'People need reassurance that life has meaning, and when all they see is confusion, lies, and stupidity, they get a sickness of the spirit which they cannot fight.'

Pendrake waited, driving on into the hills. He sensed that his quiet question had calmed the violent women in the back seat. They still held their guns, but a gesture from their commander in chief restrained them from action.

President Dayles broke the silence. 'Superficially, one might say that we suffer from immorality, corrupt politicians, and the fact that just about everybody in the country is neurotic in some way.'

Pendrake said, 'My feeling is that we suffer from a lack of leadership.' From the shocked silence in the rear seat, he surmised that his words had struck home. He went on, 'You see, Mr. President, in a democracy we elect a ruler for a limited period. That doesn't mean that he is less a ruler than any hereditary monarch. If he fails to combine spiritual and temporal guidance on a firm level, then indeed our system of government begins to decay, and we wonder what has happened. But nothing has happened except that we have elected a weakling who for reasons of his own will not give the necessary guidance.'

Dead silence, except for the hum and purr and squeak of the car.

'My feeling,' said Pendrake, 'is that it is you, Mr. President, who needs reassurance that life has meaning. So I'll make you a sporting offer.'

'An offer?' The words were not a true reaction, but more an automatic echo from a man in a deep state of shock.

'An offer,' said Pendrake quietly. 'If in three years you have given the necessary guidance and rehabilitated democracy, I will freely give you my blood.'

It was Kay who responded to that with asperity. 'I'm afraid, Mr. Pendrake, that you are not in a position to dictate when your blood will be utilized.'

'Shut up, Kay!' said Jefferson Dayles sharply.

The woman gave him an amazed look and sank back in her seat. And now she was in shock. In all their association, Pendrake realized, the man had never spoken in such a tone to this tense, beautiful, aberrated mistress of his.

President Dayles cleared his throat. 'I'm puzzled,' he said. 'We seem to have fallen in with you quite accidentally, Mr

Pendrake, but evidently you've bypassed several divisions of the American armed forces. Now I'm beginning to wonder what is really going on. For example, how did you escape from the prison?'

'You tell him, dear,' said Pendrake.

Anrella described the energy gun that Pendrake had devised.

Dayles said in amazement, 'How could he invent such a weapon from a radio?' Evidently it was a rhetorical question, for he rushed on, 'What else?' When Anrella had told him about the point of Nova-heat buried behind them in the desert sand, the President said with a gasp, 'He caused this heat wave?'My God!'

President Dayles sat very still. On his face was the look of a man who suddenly sees a solution to what has seemed an insoluble problem. He exploded, 'That's it! All of us—all of these people should be ashamed.'

'All what people?' said Anrella in astonishment.

'The just-folks type, the bar fly, the sex hunter, the muddy brains, the men-against-women, the women-against-men, the tough guys, the weaklings, the stupid, the foolish, the poor, the rich—all the degraded, angry, fearful, unhappy, dull, miserable wretches out there'—he waved vaguely, taking in half the world in his gesture—'and here' —he pointed at himself. 'All these people, preening themselves on some idiotic accomplishment that isn't an accomplishment at all, compared with what they're capable of. Three billion people have permitted the greatest brain mechanism in the universe to become wreckage, and our job is first of all to make them aware of what they've done, and then help them to untangle themselves.'

'What do you propose to do?' Anrella asked.

The great man seemed not to hear. He went on wonderingly, 'I've been puzzled about the abysmal shortage of new creative work, and the only reason for it is that man is caught up in confusion.'

He shook his head.

'I'm afraid it isn't going to be that easy,' said Anrella.

Pendrake decided it was time to stop temporizing. He said, 'I think the army should be recalled, the sentence of the condemned men commuted to five years, the equalized women unequalized, the Lambton land project protected, those involved in it freed from threat of prison, women admitted to the administrative and executive positions in greater numbers——'

Anrella's elbow struck him at that moment. 'That's enough,' she said in an angry voice. 'Jim, stop it!'

Pendrake was silent, startled. He saw that her eyes were flashing anger at him. He analyzed instantly that she knew what he was doing.

'All right,' he said slowly. 'I'll stop.' But he was astonished at her action.

Twenty-eight

It was an hour later.

The President's two cars had caught up with them, and Pendrake was assuring the Chief Executive that he could safely proceed in his own vehicle and that he and his wife would return to the ranch.

No one tried to restrain them.

As soon as they were out of sight around a bend Anrella said, 'Please stop the car!'

Pendrake was surprised but did so.

She said grimly, 'You've been using telepathic hypnotism.'

'So?' He was unconcerned.

'This!' She had been fumbling in her purse. Now she brought out a tiny flashlight. It burned at him with an intense light. The light seemed attuned to something in his brain, for it hurt him deep inside his head. Involuntarily Pendrake cried out.

He was aware of her saying something, but he didn't really hear the words. She stopped finally. There was a pause. Then he heard her say, 'You haven't got that ability any more.'

Pendrake sat there blinking. He seemed completely conscious and unhurt. He stared at her. 'You hypnotized me mechanically?' he said accusingly.

'No. I merely changed a brain pattern.' She was firm. 'Jim, it's really very simple. We can't have someone in the group, or in the world, with the ability to influence others without their being aware of it.'

'I used it only to re-establish democracy, as you saw.'

'Democracy has to work out its own salvation,' she said sharply. 'It can only move as fast as the people.'

Pendrake said in amazement, 'That's a strange statement from the real leader of the Lambton project.'

'We learned our lesson,' she said bitterly. 'Private individuals cannot supersede their government. No small group within a state can set itself up in a superior moral position. We have nearly eight hundred dead, Jim, and if we don't get government help the entire Lambton settlement on Venus will be taken over by those East Germans. They know where we are.'

'That won't happen.' Pendrake shook his head and explained about the expedition President Dayles had authorized to go to the moon. Then he said 'Anrella, I need weapons and a speedy lift to a certain cliffside in the Middle West. I've got to make a jump through space to the moon.'

He described where, and how, and what the situation was.

Anrella's eyes were wide when he had finished. 'I'll call the spaceship,' she said quickly. Then, 'But why not wait a day or so until we can get some of our young men to go with you? You may need help.'

Pendrake thought of Eleanor and shook his head. 'I've been filled with rage and horror ever since the memory came. Send them after me, but I can't wait.'

She stared straight ahead, a strained expression on her face. Finally, softly, 'I understand, Jim.'

On the way, he told her about the moon people and concluded, 'It fits with what you said. The refuge they offered me was so far out of my reality that I chose to take my chances against a saber-toothed tiger. Evidently man is somewhere in the late beast stage all mixed in with awareness of the first really human stage, which is barely beginning to manifest. In my toti-potent phases I showed what the untrammeled human brain as it now is *could* be like. But I sense that the brain is still evolving. What we will be able to understand when it has gone through its next change may have no relation to the way we are now.'

The conversation ended as the missile-ship arrived at the spot in midair above the highway. There was a brief maneuvering under Pendrake's direction, and then it was time to say good-by.

'Don't worry!' said Anrella as she kissed him. 'I was lucky to have you at all, and I surrender you freely to your Eleanor. We'll meet again.'

Firmly Pendrake moved to the door and then down the steps that had been lowered from the ship. The last step hung directly opposite the flow point. Standing on it, he probed forward tentatively, watched his hand disappear, and then confidently stepped into what seemed empty air.

There was the same sense of being in a black fog that he remembered from before. The next instant——

Something as hard as rock struck him on the head, and with a crash he fell to the metal floor.

That was his final awareness before unconsciousness closed over him.

Twenty-nine

Pendrake came to at some indeterminate time later.

His hands were bound behind his back. Standing over him was Big Oaf.

The scene around them was terrifyingly familiar. There, a few feet away, was the cliff's edge.

The Neanderthal chuckled hoarsely. He was obviously in a state of glee. 'Now I kin relax. All these months you've given me a turn, an' I let Devlin an' his men have that second town 'cause I wasn't sure what you were doin'. Course, I fixed this little rig here to sock you one if you ever showed up. Now I gotcha. Now I kin go after them 'n' knock 'em off one by one till they come yellin' for mercy.'

He paused for breath; then, 'We're gonna pick up right where we left off, Pendrake. The devil-beast gets you, and believe me, I ain't wastin' no time.'

Pendrake stared up at the man. His strength was coming back, but that was meaningless now. He had made his last of many mistakes, and in a few minutes now *finis* would be written to the career of James Pendrake.

For a flashing moment he was amazed to realize how vulnerable human beings really were. Actually without his toti-potency, he would by now be either dead or so crippled by so many amputations that the mental picture of it made him quail. The truth was that people who took physical risks could not survive for long.

The thought ended and was gone. He saw that the creature-man was grinning at him and that the monster trembled with what had all the appearance of a tremendous sadistic excitement.

Pendrake found his voice. 'Big Oaf,' he said, but there was little conviction in his voice, 'the United States armed forces will be landing on the moon within a week, and another force of a thousand men will be coming through this machine in the next week. I came ahead to talk to you and to get your co-operation. You kill me—and you'll be executed within seven days. They'll give you a military trial and hang you.'

'Shurrup!' the small eyes glared at him. 'You ain't talkin' yourself outta nuthin', Pendrake. I've bin waiting for you, but nobody else ain't comin' through this machine again. Soon as I get you out'n the way I'm gonna blow it up. An' as for any army diggin' their way down here—it'd take 'em years even if they knew which way to dig. I'll lay you a hunnerd to one they ain't got any real diggin' stuff with 'em——' He broke off. 'What's gonna happen here is between you 'n' me. No one else knows nuthin' about it. Devlin thinks you're dead. What else kin he think, seein' as you ain't bin around fer months?'

Pendrake had to agree. This murderous little episode was strictly between Big Oaf, himself, and the giant beast in the pit far below.

The Neanderthal continued gloatingly, 'You can see the way the machine is set only a few feet from the edge of the cliff. There was a time when everythin' that came through ran right over the edge, and its straight down here—nuthin' to grab onto till you get a long way down. I was just walkin', so I was able to jump back, but the devil-beast an' a lot of the animals it lived on till I came must have been runnin' down that trail on Earth.

'After I built that corral barrier, I could save all the deer and buffalo and cattle that came through, an' I fed the beast the leavin's, I always fed it myself, so now it knows my call. Lissen!'

He walked to the cliff's edge and uttered a low, piercing cry. For a moment then he stood staring down, facing away from Pendrake. He was crouching, slightly bow-legged, and he seemed suddenly like the living embodiment of man's bestial heritage, a squat, hairy, inhuman shape, a man-thing spawned at the dawn of prehistory, a creature out of a hideous, almost impossible dream, and yet truly he was man's ancestor, and some vestige of him lurked within the breast cage of every modern man.

But for a few instants of eternity he *was* facing away.

Shaking in every nerve, shedding tiny rivers of perspiration, Pendrake slid forward on his back.

Big Oaf turned. 'He's comin',' he said. He seemed not to notice the strained body, the strained expression on his captive's face. He said in a matter-of-fact tone that was more terrible than all the passion and fury that had gone before, 'I'm gonna let you slide down on a rope, untyin' the bonds around your wrists just before I lower you over the edge. That way you'll be able to do a little runnin' when you get down. The beast likes that; it gives him exercise.'

There was a rope neatly coiled at one side of the cave. As he picked it up and tossed one end over the abyss, Big Oaf explained, 'I keep this here handy. You ain't the first, you know, who's gone over secret like this. Notice how one end's tied to this corral post? Funny,' he soliloquized, 'the kind of stuff the men have brought with 'em from Earth : rope, a wagonload of tools, dynamite, rifles, revolvers—I got 'em all. Some of it, mostly ammunition, is hid in this cave, an' the rest in other caves they don't know about that I closed up.

'I'm gonna use those guns on Devlin. It don't take long to kill a hunnerd men from ambush if you got bullets.

'You see,' he finished with a grin, 'I got it all figgered.'

Pendrake scrambled to his feet and raced straight at the monster. Big Oaf stopped and, snarling, waited, great arms reaching. Pendrake leaped, but it was the leap of a jumper, feet first. His hard shoes struck at stomach level with a full two hundred pounds of his weight behind it, and Big Oaf sat down.

As Pendrake fell, helpless because of his bound arms, he used foot leverage and flung himself away from the reaching arms, rolled madly—and once against made it to his feet.

Big Oaf stood up shakily and growled, 'Ye're tough, Pendrake, but that pretty footwork don't get you no chips in this game.'

Silently, earnestly, Pendrake raced at his powerful enemy in a dead run. He had no illusions. It was all or nothing. And it had to be right now, before Big Oaf recovered whatever strength he had lost from the 'pretty footwork.'

The Neanderthal was braced for more footwork, and so what followed had another small element of surprise. With the full thrust of his body, Pendrake smashed head-on against that bulging form.

Big Oaf staggered back and simultaneously grabbed with apelike arms, and with a yell of triumph successfully embraced Pendrake. 'Gotcha!' he roared.

With all the strength in his legs, Pendrake fought to keep going forward.

And it was enough strength.

So great was the momentum of that run, and of that shove, that Big Oaf stayed off balance and kept moving back toward the cliff's edge.

Pendrake said, 'We're going over together.'

The truth of that must have dawned on the monster at that penultimate moment, because he cried out, a piercing cry. Then he did what a person who is on the point of falling over a cliff does automatically—he let go of Pendrake and grabbed at the corral post.

Pendrake shoved at him without mercy, and Big Oaf, squealing like a stuck pig, went over the edge of the cliff.

Thirty

Pendrake leaned on the corral post and sagged there, gasping. Finally, as his strength trickled back, he peered over the edge of the cliff.

Big Oaf was getting to his feet on the grass below, and cautiously circling him was the saber-toothed tiger. As Pendrake stared. Big Oaf began to back away from the animal. That was normal enough.

It was the sabertooth that was acting abnormal. The great tiger was whining in unmistakable puzzlement—*and backing away from the hairy man.*

Backing away—it couldn't be fear. Nothing alive on Earth in the last ten million years could have brought one tremor of fear to that savage heart.

Big Oaf was shaking his head like a stunned person, and Pendrake's attention concentrated on the man, even as the animal darted out of sight.

He saw that the Neanderthal was heading for the rope that hung down from the cave.

With a quick movement, using his feet, Pendrake pulled the rope out of his reach.

'Pendrake!'

The squat body was directly below. The unsightly head turned fearfully toward the spot where the tiger had disappeared; then, 'Pendrake, it musta recognized me as its feeder, but it'll be back. Pendrake, let that rope down.'

Pendrake felt no mercy. His body was ice-cold from the freezing thoughts that were in his mind. His whole being throbbed. He said, 'Go to all the hells you've ever sent other men to. Lie in the belly of the beast you've nurtured with the bodies of your victims. May the god who made you have pity on you; I have none.'

'I'll promise anything.'

His rage did not lessen. It grew. A picture came of the women who must have shuddered at the very sight of, let alone the touch of, the monstrosity who was now pleading with a human voice for the mercy it had never shown to anyone. He thought of Eleanor——

His mind chilled to a new depth of steely will. 'Promises,' he mocked, and his laughter re-echoed over that ancient valley of the long-dead moon.

And ended——

There was a flicker of yellow-red-blue-green in the brush a hundred yards to the right. A moment before, Pendrake had longed for the return of the mighty killer. But now—revulsion came swift to emotions that had been plucked raw. Horror flashed along his nerves. 'I'm mad,' he thought. 'One man can't administer justice. Letting another human being go to a death like this. After all, it isn't a true parallel.'

He kicked at the rope. It dropped straight down. 'Quick!' he cried. 'We can talk when you're out of reach of——'

The rope sagged with weight; Pendrake watched the desperate man in his fight for life. The tiger was pacing wildly, watching the swaying body above him in an obvious fever of excitement. It kept looking up with eyes of yellow fire, roaring uneasily and with an unmistakable gathering awareness of escaping food. Suddenly, whatever tie had held it back, whatever tie of fantastically ancient companionship had bound it to the man, snapped.

It ran back, then turned toward the cliff again and became a streak of blazing color against the gray-brown walls. A hundred, a hundred and fifty, a hundred and eighty feet it raced up that perpendicular wall. And missed. It seemed as if the miss were no more than a few feet.

Down, down, the animal went. As it reached the bottom, it whirled and with what seemed a reasoned calculation made a run to the far end of the compound and came back at enormous speed. Once more it catapulted up the steep cliff. This time it missed only by inches.

But it *was* a miss.

When it tumbled down the second time, it made no further effort. It simply sat there on its haunches, watching its almost-prey climb out of range.

From above, Pendrake looked down at the sweating, struggling, swaying figure. He was uneasy but determined. When Big Oaf was ten feet away he said, 'All right, that's far enough.'

The other stopped instantly and looked up pleadingly. 'Pendrake, don't push me down there again. We'll have a democracy. We'll free the women. They can choose.'

Pendrake said, 'Toss your knife up here.'

An instant later the knife curved through the air and landed on the metal floor fifteen feet behind him.

'Now,' said Pendrake, 'lower yourself about thirty feet. I'll need that much time to get the knife.'

Big Oaf promptly but carefully slid down a full forty feet. 'I tell you, Pendrake, you got my co-operation.'

Pendrake secured the knife and came to the edge of the precipice. It took him many minutes to manipulate the blade with his bound hands and so cut the cords that held him. But when the job was done he felt better, more confident, more convinced that all was going to be well.

He waited precious minutes while he re-established the circulation in his wrists and fingers; and then——

'Climb up here!' he commanded the Neanderthal.

Big Oaf hauled himself up to within feet of the edge. 'Stop!' Pendrake ordered.

The other poised uneasily. 'Whatcha gonna do?' he gasped.

Pendrake said, 'Loop the rope around you so that it's supporting your weight without your having to hold on.'

Eagerly Big Oaf looped and twisted and successfully created a rope seat for himself.

'Now, hold up your hands; I'm going to tie them,' said Pendrake.

When that was done, Pendrake said slowly, 'All right, Big Oaf, I am now going to ask you the key question. What happened to my wife?'

The creature breathed hard. 'She's all right, fella,' he mumbled. 'Devlin got her from my joint that day he attacked. Some say there's a guy courtin' her, but she's waitin'. She says nuthin' can kill a feller like you.'

A warm glow spread through Pendrake's whole body. 'Good old Eleanor,' he thought. He said, 'Big Oaf, I'm going to pull you up and then I'm going to take you down to the village.'

'You ain't gonna turn me over to those fellers tied like this?' The Neanderthal was instantly in a panic.

'I'm not turning you over to anyone,' Pendrake said patiently. 'We'll tear down your stockade and give you a place in the community like any other person. Big, tough guys have become good citizens before.'

As he drew the man up over the cliff's edge to safety, it struck him that man everywhere was still grappling with his primitive heritage. Somehow, on the vast scale of international existence and in the arena of national power, it was almost impossible to cage the savage beast. But here, in the limited world of a small population, it could probably be achieved—if the way to Earth were left open and if secret contact were maintained through, for example, Anrella's group.

There were many ifs. And because he was doubtful, because man had nowhere solved these problems, and because here on the moon he wanted no failures, Pendrake paused with his prisoner in the cave room with the intense blue light and the transparent cube, where the moon people maintained what was left of their strange life.

Into the center of the light he spoke silently. 'Am I doing the right thing?'

He sighed with frustration as the answer came into his brain: 'Friend, the universe of illusions to which you have oriented yourself has no right.'

Pendrake tried again: 'But there must be levels of rightness. Within the limited frame where I operate, am I being wise?'

'The material universe,' came the reply, 'is a momentary—in terms of eternity—attempt at differentiation, but the basic truth is that everything equals everything else.'

That shocked Pendrake. He said in a complete surprise, '*All* differences are illusions?'

'All.'

'There is only oneness?' he demanded.

'Forever.'

Pendrake swallowed and became stubborn. 'But, then, what is the manyness that we perceive?'

'Illusionary weak and strong energy signals.'

'But who are they signaling to?'

'To each other.'

Momentarily Pendrake felt blank, but he was still not satisfied. Nevertheless, his tone was bitter as he asked, 'If this be true, why have you taken the form that you now have, and continue to exist?'

'The answer to that is the secret that man must slowly and painfully evolve to. But this is also transitory, the result of our own departure from eternal truth. Long before we can return to what is, we shall welcome you to—oneness.'

'I won't be here,' said Pendrake grimly. 'Man's life is short, no matter how he pants for immortality.'

'No signal is ever lost,' was the calm reply, 'for all signals are one.'

Pendrake could think of no answer to that, and it was obvious that these meta-Socratic analyses had no message for him. 'Good-by,' was all he said.

Silence answered.

Within the hour Eleanor's soft kiss made meaningless for Pendrake all that the moon people had said. For she was in *his* arms and not in someone else's; it was toward him that she—signaled—an intense emotion of love . . .

Other developments in the moon community were also highly individual in nature.

Not too surprisingly, in view of what Big Oaf had once said, one of the creature-man's wives actually did choose to stay married to him. The Neanderthal himself seemed resigned to being an ordinary citizen. This was particularly noticeable after the stockade was torn down. It was then he revealed where he had hidden the ammunition and other valuable materials.

Such actions seemed to point to a much more peaceful future.

As Pendrake explained it to Eleanor, 'We may not quickly find out what life is. Maybe we'll never know what the moon people think they discovered. But if we get a police force operating here under a system of law, we'll have time to get those super-machines working without fear that someone will use them against us. For that, the Lambton people will be our best collaborators. After that—well, we'll do what's rational.'

Eleanor wanted to know, shudderingly, 'What about that awful beast in the pit?'

Pendrake smiled, 'I think I know exactly how we'll eventually handle the sabertooth. You'll see.'

The winter clung. The snow seemed determined to stay forever. When it finally dissipated, the new, glistening, all-plastic Interplanetary Building was opened with a triumphant fanfare, and the great appointment had already come to Hoskins: Commissioner—Chairman——

'It is absolutely unfair,' he said to Cree Lipton, 'that I should have this. There are a dozen men who laid the groundwork and fought in obscurity. Frankly, I accepted only when I heard that the notorious Governor Cartwright, who was defeated in the last elections, was gunning for the job as a sort of pension for services rendered the party.'

'I wouldn't worry about it,' Lipton said. 'You can help those people more than they could ever help themselves. By the way, did you see the announcement about Venus? Recognition for the Lambton colony there as a United Nations first-degree mandate, with Venusian citizenship already given a special first-class status. Professor Grayson and the other scientists and their families didn't die in vain.'

Hoskins nodded. 'It's a great victory.'

He was interrupted: 'Listen, Ned, what I really came to see you about—— Put on your hat, come with me.'

Hoskins shook his head, smiling. 'Impossible, old man. The reports from our successful expedition to the moon are just reaching the flood stage. There's one really curious item——'

He took a folder from a drawer and flipped over several pages of foolscap. '"The Nazi prisoners claim," ' he read, ' "that they were captured easily because their military forces had for months been engaged in digging along collapsed tunnels, trying to root out some creatures who live inside the moon. They claim that these beings are human. Our investigations have found only caves that sooner or later came to a dead end." '

He saw that Lipton was looking at his watch. The FBI agent caught his glance and apologized. 'I'm sorry to break in on you, but the zero hour is approaching, and we shall just have time to fly to New York and be in at the kill.'

Hoskins gasped, 'You don't mean——' He leaped to his

feet, grabbed his hat and coat. 'Come on. Let's go!'

When the uproar started the stocky man glanced sharply at the leader.

'Excellency——' he began.

He stopped as he saw that the gaunt man was sitting with the phone still in his fingers, staring straight ahead. Uneasily Birdman watched as the receiver dropped from the other's fingers, watched as the man sat there, his face like a dark, lifeless mask.

Birdman ventured, 'Excellency, you were saying just before the phone lights came on that now that our positions on the moon and nearly all our engines have been captured we would use those that escaped as a nucleus for piratical depredations on the interplanetary highways that will now be opened up. We would become, you said, the pirates of the twenty-first century. We——'

He stopped, frozen in horror. The long, bony fingers of the leader were groping in a desk drawer. They came out holding a Mauser automatic.

As Lipton and Hoskins and a dozen other men burst into the room, the stocky man was on his feet, facing the spare-built man at the desk, who was raising a revolver to his own forehead.

'Excellency,' Birdman was crying wildly, 'you lied. You *are* afraid, too.'

The pistol blared, and the gaunt man twisted in his brief agony and slid to the floor. Birdman stood over him with a numb terror; he felt but dimly the presence of the intruders.

As he was led away there was in him only wave after wave of disillusionment.

It was a spring morning five years later. Len Christopher, assistant keeper, New York Greater Zoological Gardens, walked slowly along the line of big cat cages. Suddenly he stopped and stared at a vast, metal-barred structure that glittered in the rays of the rising sun.

'Funny,' he muttered, 'I swear that wasn't there last night. Wonder when it arri——'

He stopped. The top of his head made a valiant effort to unfasten from the rest of him. For a moment he stood gaping at the blue-green-yellow-red nightmare that loomed colossal behind the four-inch metal bars. And then——

Then he was running, yelling, for the superintendent's office.

In one small area the .. beast ... was caged.

THE WORLD'S GREATEST NOVELISTS
NOW AVAILABLE IN PANTHER BOOKS

Ernest Hemingway

The Old Man and The Sea	50p	☐
Fiesta	75p	☐
For Whom the Bell Tolls	90p	☐
A Farewell to Arms	75p	☐
The Snows of Kilimanjaro	60p	☐
The Essential Hemingway	£1.25	☐
To Have and Have Not	75p	☐
Death in the Afternoon (Non-Fiction)	£1.25	☐
Green Hills of Africa	75p	☐
Men Without Women	75p	☐
A Moveable Feast	75p	☐
The Torrents of Spring	75p	☐
Across the River and Into the Trees	75p	☐
Winner Take Nothing	80p	☐

Richard Hughes

A High Wind in Jamaica	60p	☐
In Hazard	60p	☐

James Joyce

Dubliners	75p	☐
A Portrait of the Artist as a Young Man	75p	☐
Stephen Hero	£1.25	☐
The Essential James Joyce	£1.50	☐

TRUE CRIME – NOW AVAILABLE IN PANTHER BOOKS

TRUE ADVENTURE – NOW AVAILABLE IN PANTHER BOOKS

Kenneth Ainslie

Pacific Ordeal   75p ☐

Henri Charriere

Papillon   £1.25 ☐
Banco   85p ☐

Emmett Grogan

Ringolevio   95p ☐

Henri de Monfreid

Smuggling Under Sail in the Red Sea   75p ☐

Wyn Sargent

My Life with the Headhunters   60p ☐

Andre Voisin

Don Fernando   75p ☐

THE WORLD'S GREATEST NOVELISTS
NOW AVAILABLE IN PANTHER BOOKS

John O'Hara

Ourselves to Know	60p	☐
Ten North Frederick	50p	☐
A Rage to Live	60p	☐

Norman Mailer

The Fight (Non-Fiction)	75p	☐
The Presidential Papers	95p	☐
Barbary Shore	40p	☐
Advertisements for Myself	50p	☐
An American Dream	£1.25	☐
The Naked and The Dead	£1.50	☐

Kingsley Amis

Ending Up	60p	☐
The Riverside Villas Murder	95p	☐
I Like It Here	50p	☐
That Uncertain Feeling	50p	☐
Girl 20	40p	☐
I Want It Now	60p	☐
The Green Man	95p	☐

All these book are available at your local bookshop or newsagent, or can be ordered direct from the publisher. Just tick the titles you want and fill in the form below.

Name ....

Address ....

....

Write to Panther Cash Sales, PO Box 11, Falmouth, Cornwall TR10 9EN.

Please enclose remittance to the value of the cover price plus:

UK: 22p for the first book plus 10p per copy for each additional book ordered to a maximum charge of 82p.

BFPO and EIRE: 22p for the first book plus 10p per copy for the next 6 books, thereafter 3p per book.

OVERSEAS: 30p for the first book and 10p for each additional book.

Granada Publishing reserve the right to show new retail prices on covers, which may differ from those previously advertised in the text or elsewhere.